Leaving *Jade*

SHANIQUA SNOWDEN

Published by Snowden Books

Photo used on book cover by Sashkin

Printed in the United States

ISBN: 978-0615952154

CONTENTS

ACKNOWLEDGMENTS

First and foremost I would like to thank my Lord and Savior Jesus Christ. This book couldn't have been possible if it weren't by the Grace of God. I truly enjoy writing and it's a passion I plan to continue to do forever. I would also like to thank my husband, the love of my life and my very best friend, who is my greatest supporter. Another person I'd like to thank is my mom, another one of my greatest supporters. Thank you for believing in me mom. A thank you also goes out to my dad. And thank you so much for those of you who are reading. I am honored that you would support me and pick up one of my books to read. I hope you be richly blessed by reading it. Thank you!

Chapter 1

It was another day, another dollar. Audrey Mitchell, or Jade, her street name what most knew her by, made her way down the worn and rugged cracked sidewalk that she was so familiar with on Lankford Avenue, searching for the best spot to score a large jackpot that night. The night was breezy, but not cold enough to where she needed a jacket, which was in her favor so she could reveal to the potential johns who were riding by what they were in a treat for if they decided to pay for her services. She wore a tightfitting red mini dress that didn't leave too much to the imagination. Not to seem boastful about it, but she knew how to use her physical assets for her gain. She was tall, curvy and slender, and had seemingly endless legs that ran for miles. From just one bat of her long, arched eye lashes men would succumb to her.

A few newbies were on the opposite side of the street trying to flag down every car they saw zooming past them. So ignorant and young, those girls were on a fast track to landing themselves right inside of a jail cell. Although there were a few close calls, out of her eleven years being in the business Audrey never once got busted by the cops, something she kind of prided herself about.

Being in the game for so long she knew how to lure customers in without being inordinately obvious about it. The way she subtly rocked her hips from side to side while sauntering down the streets was enough to make heads turn and cars stop for her.

While her mind wandered her legs led her down the littered, narrow streets to the corner she referred to as her lucky spot. Though it happened rarely, it was there she could earn at least six hundred dollars per night and sometimes as high up in the thousands. All the money would go right into her hands and she wouldn't have to worry about paying a penny worth of incalculable taxes. When she got to her haven she was happy to find it was uninhabited by any of the other girls. She leaned her back against one of the streetlamps and extended her chest outwards. So far she'd only saw a couple of cars passing by; the drivers all eyeing her up and down to compare was she better than the previous women they'd passed. If she were better they wouldn't hesitate to do a U-turn after checking out the other sellers further up the street and approach her. From the few cars driving through, tonight didn't seem like it was going to be such a busy night. Maybe the husbands, who were a major customer base, were with their wives and children tonight to make up for their guilty conscious. After the act was done and over with they'd always try to give Audrey a story that would justify their cheating ways, but she could care less about their sorry excuses. All she needed for them to do was to compensate her so she could get back to her post for other paying customers. She had to keep the cash flowing—the simple reason being because she had bills to pay and they weren't going to just pay for themselves.

It never interested her to know things personal about her customers or to ask those questions regarding who they were; their likes and dislikes. Altogether she didn't like knowing anything about them. And what she hated the most was to find out they were husbands, which their wedding rings gave away—you'd think they'd take them off before seeking her services. Learning they were husbands further diminished whatever hope she might've had left in men. From all she encountered of men they were like ravaging beast who craved the flesh of women. They were all no good dirty dogs— actually comparing them to dogs was an insult to the dogs. She rested her head back on the street lamp, guessing that made her somewhat of a hypocrite for using their weaknesses for her gain, but she had to make ends meet in this dark, cruel world somehow. And men sure didn't mind using her for their gain.

Down the street she spotted a tall and scrawny looking almond toned man, appearing to be in his mid to late twenties, approaching her way. His long-sleeved, light blue collared shirt was tucked deep inside of his tan dress pants that stopped a couple of inches above his ankles, revealing his bulky white long socks. His ensemble was paired off with some white sneakers. He was the epitome of what one would call a dork. The only thing he was missing was some bifocals. This sad man probably found his way to the streets looking for some pleasure after being rejected by so many women. She stood straight and pulled up her bra straps to give her bust some extra lift and volume, readying herself to make her first transaction for the night.

Chapter 2

He parked his vehicle a few blocks down from his destination, got out of the car with his Bible in hand, and made sure all of his doors were locked. Where he was wasn't exactly a safe place to be at. Jason Goodman couldn't believe he was on Lankford Avenue; a notorious place in Tampa, Florida for all kinds of crimes and wickedness, about to witness to prostitutes—or at least attempt to anyhow. Outreaching wasn't his thing he admitted. He remembered the reason he was there to begin with, the words of his Pastor ranging freshly in his ears…

"Jason, my boy. Do you know why I called you into my office

today?" Pastor James set his elbows atop his vast cherry wood desk, squinting his eyes at him through his black rimmed rectangle glasses, ready to give him some sort of lecture Jason could tell—again.

He'd been in Pastor James's church office an innumerable amount of times that by now he could draw it from memory. The grand cherry desk was placed at the center of the spacious room with stacks of papers spread neatly across the left edge. Sometimes his laptop would be open on the right side of him, like it was today. There was a grand bookshelf placed on the wall behind his desk that held a wide range of books about Christianity and leadership. The office had a small gray filing cabinet in a corner, a mini black refrigerator and one medium sized window that was always closed and covered by silk brown drapery with gold embroidery. The ceiling fixture provided enough light to dimly illuminate the whole room. Other than that there were no other decorations or personal materials, well aside from this one bright orange umbrella shaped glass lamp that stood out against the neutral colors of the room. It was always turned off on a wicker table, having no purpose for being there.

"No sir." Jason responded. But he knew whatever he'd been called into his office for it wasn't for a good reason, because it never was.

"If you want to elevate to the position of executive pastor I need to see more out of you." He clasped his large hands together with the same stern look on his aged chestnut toned face Jason was so accustomed to him displaying. His voice held authority and decisiveness. It was the same tone he used to preach every Sunday morning during his sermons. As the Senior and Founding Pastor over Waters of Life, who'd built the church with his own blood, sweat and tears, he demanded respect, and Jason did respect him, but he couldn't quite follow where his words were coming from.

"Well, what do you mean by that sir?" Jason asked him. Wasn't he already showing his capabilities with all of the responsibilities he had in the church; ranging from being over three different ministries (that he ran successfully he might add) and basically being on Pastor James's beck and call whenever he needed him for anything.

"You do well with managing things and getting things done, yes, but I don't know about you being relational with others. Many people have come to me recently telling me how you're unfriendly and unapproachable, that you're in a league all of your own. If you want to become a pastor of the people, helping them and building relationships with them should be your number one priority and concern."

Taking a small breath inside Jason struggled to refrain from showing the astonishment he was feeling to manifest through his face. The only people who could be coming to tattle or make up slanders about him were the ones who wanted the position for themselves, and he had an idea of just who those people might be. Pastor James being so quick to believe in their words was also another let down, he more than likely held the same sentiments regarding Jason as his accusers did.

"I thought getting things done does help the people." He replied as politely as he could.

Pastor James removed his glasses while closing his eyes, looking as if he were getting weary of Jason's rebuttals.

"You're not understanding." he shook his head. "Ministry is more than just the inside of these four walls and getting assignments done, my boy. When was the last time you brought someone to Christ outside of this building or opened up your home to a stranger?"

He waited for Jason to reply, but seeing he had no answer continued speaking in his arbitrative tone. "You don't know how to reach people. When you start caring more for the lost, who are out in the world dying not only internally, but externally, then we can talk about you possibly becoming the new executive pastor." He put back on his glasses and gave Jason a firm look that told him he was done with the conversation.

Just he wait and see. Jason was going to show him exactly how "relational" he could be with people and how he could win anyone over to Christ, even the filthiest of sinners. That's how he found his way here on Lankford Avenue. Who could be more abhorrent than a prostitute?

The dorky man reached her on the sidewalk looking uptight with an unbending frown on his face.

Could the reason why he be so uncomfortable was because he had a wife at home waiting for him?

She glanced at his ring finger to find that it was ring less, though he could've taken it off before he'd gotten there. If he wasn't married then maybe the reason why he was so uptight was because it was his first time seeking for a prostitute. She'd gotten a few types of those men before. If that was the case then Audrey knew just what to do to ease his nerves.

"Hey there, suga." she smiled alluringly while folding her arms. "What can I do for you tonight?" She swung her well-rounded hips to the side.

Jason examined her. She reminded him of a light, brown skinned version of Jessica off of the movie *Who Framed Roger the Rabbit*. He'd watched that movie when he was ten-years-old thinking it was going to be an innocent child's movie because of the cartoon characters, but was surprised to see the adult themes the movie had laced in it. He couldn't exactly remember all of what the movie was about, but what he could remember was that immodest woman character vividly. The lady standing in front of him was provocative just like her, revealing her cleavage and having her body out on full display. She had long wavy and kinky black hair that blew lightly in the wind. Her make-up was applied augmenting her facial features; with her thin ebony arched eyebrows, full red glossy lips, smoky brown eyes, and contoured check bones. Everything about her was enticing yet repulsive. Before coming he'd already prepared himself for her enchantress ways. He wasn't going to fall like Adam did to temptation. Jason was well aware how the devil made evil things come in beautiful packages so that he could entrap people, just like she was trying to do to him now.

"What you can do for me is accept Jesus as your Lord and Savior and repent of your sinful ways." He said bluntly.

Suppressing her astonishment Audrey gave out a slight guffaw. She looked down at his hands, just now noticing he was holding a brown leather Bible. Was this man joking with her right now, because she didn't have the time for his jokes?

"Mister, my starting rate is at fifty dollars. Now that being established either you tell me what you want or you can leave me alone with all of your Jesus talk." She said it with assertiveness, but at the same time holding civility in her vocalization.

She didn't want to come off as too aggressive. For all she knew this guy could be a deranged man and go all wacko on her. The people who roamed these streets were thugs, drug addicts, robbers and convicts of all the sorts. Those types of people didn't care who you were. If you were in their way of getting what they wanted or if you had something they wanted they'd take it from you by force, even if they had to go as far as killing you to get it. Audrey had learned the ropes of life on the streets early on and how to stay alive.

"Well, that's what I want from you is to accept Jesus. He's much better than this filthy life you're living." Jason looked at her up and down distastefully. It was dreadful how she was wrecking her life without a care.

Audrey felt herself beginning to lose patience with the dorky man. Not only was he trying to preach to her, but furthermore he was insulting her too.

"How about going to preach to someone else why don't cha? Didn't you see any other girls on your way while walking down here to try to convert or whatever?"

"No, I didn't. You were the first one that I saw."

Well that was just dandy for her. Audrey rolled her eyes. That meant all of her probable consumers were going to the girls further down the street. So far her usually lucky spot tonight was only bringing her misfortune.

"All the same, you can still leave me alone. I'm not interested in whatever you're trying to sell."

"I'm not trying to sell you anything. I'm telling you that you need Jesus." Jason wasn't going to back down. He was set on showing Pastor James he could win a soul no matter how hopeless they were.

Before she could argue with him any longer a white beat up car drove up and made a stop in front of them. The potbellied man let down his window peering up at Audrey, his face round and oiled with his body sweat. "Hey, how much do you charge?" Nothing about the man was attractive to her, but business was business and she'd had much worse looking customers before.

Jason looked over his shoulder at the overweight man. On his plump face was longing and eagerness. He didn't seem embarrassed at all to be inquiring about such heinous things. Jason wasn't about to allow this unlawfulness to transpire on his watch.

"She is busy with me at the moment." Jason told him.

"Could you just leave me alone?" Audrey said growing ever the more frustrated with the dorky man.

"Huh?" The man in the car looked at her confused.

"Oh, no I'm not talking about you suga. This man here is just being an annoying pest." She stepped closer to his car, but the dorky man extended his arm out in front of her, blocking her way and wouldn't move aside.

Jason ignored her and looked grimly into the man's face. "You should just go on home now and ask God to forgive you for your indecent ways."

"Don't listen to him suga." She implored to the man in the car, attempting to keep her only customer she'd had so far for the entire night.

"It'd be best if you did listen to me." Jason told the man coldly.

"Ok, I don't need this." The man rode away offended.

"Look, I told you to leave me alone already didn't I? Now you're losing me my money." Her voice rose. She wasn't trying to be courteous with him any longer.

"Money? Is money all that important to you?"

"Well, it keeps clothes on my back."

"You mean it barely keeps clothes on your back." Jason said with a frown, having to keep his eyes anywhere other than below her face, fearing he would've committed a sin just by glancing at her minimal covered body.

"And what does it profit a man—or woman in this case, to gain it all, but to lose her very soul?" The dorky man held up his Bible. "That's a scripture here in the Word of God." He then began flipping through the pages to find the verse so he could read it to her.

"You don't have to waste your time showing me. I'll have you know that I'm well versed on plenty of scripture." She cut her eyes at him. In the process from the corner of her eye she saw a sleek black car stealthily making its way down the streets. She quickly took a double take. She'd seen cars like that on a regular basis through these parts. How it was taking its time pulling up on them, she knew for a fact it was an undercover police car.

A smile crept across her lips at the idea of leaving the dorky man alone to get busted on the streets, payback for him losing her a client, but then her conscious started pricking at her making her feel bad about the thought. Why Audrey had to have a conscious she didn't know.

"Look." she said with reluctance. "If you don't want to land in the dog pin tonight follow my lead. There's an undercover cop coming towards us at twelve O'clock."

Jason clutched the Bible in his hands tighter, alarmed. This could not go on his clean and innocent record. All he could think about was the executive pastor position falling from his grasp.

"Don't look!" She told him as he was about to turn his head to see.

He did as informed and kept his focus on the Bible he was holding. Here he was trying to do something good and was about to get into trouble for it. He did a silent prayer to the Lord that He would get him out of this somehow.

"I could just tell them I was witnessing to you, which is the truth." He said trying to remain cool.

The woman looked at him like he was naïve.

"Yeah, they're really going to believe you when you tell them that. Just follow me or choose the slammer, your choice."

The sound of her heels clicked as she walked away. Jason, not being able to fathom what was going on followed her lead.

Audrey had rehearsed this scenario countless of times so it wasn't a big deal for her. She could tell from the dorky man's expression that he was terrified. She smiled to herself feeling like she'd gotten a little repayment back from earlier.

As the enchantress led the way he couldn't help but to feel like he was being led to his doom. She stopped not far away from the spot they'd left moments ago in front of a brick wall. She then moved aside a thin board that was camouflaged in with the wall.

It revealed a narrow, long alleyway that scantly had enough standing room for the both of them. She went in first.

"Well, what are you waiting for? Get in?" She beckoned him over with her hand after seeing he wasn't moving fast enough.

He slid his body in the tiny space. His back was pressed closely against the chilled wall allowing there to be some distance between he and the enchantress—the more space the better. They were head to head with one another. She was pretty tall maybe five-foot-seven or eight, but naturally he would've been taller than her by a few inches or so if it weren't for her ridiculous stripper, high heel shoes she was wearing.

The dorky man looked anywhere other than her face like he'd rather be anywhere else besides where he was right now with her. His creamy skin glistened in the moonlight. He had a square shaped face, black curly short haircut with his sides being cut lower than the top, a clean shaven face, and clear maple brown eyes. Seeing him from up close like this, he actually looked pretty cute for a dork. She could see the beads of sweat forming on his forehead.

"Relax, you have nothing to worry about. They'll soon pass on by." She smiled charmingly.

"How can I relax in a situation like this?" She might've been used to living this kind of low life, but Jason wasn't.

"Be thankful I didn't take you to the dumpster instead to hide there. It's much better hiding here suga."

"Do you call everybody "suga"?"

"No, just the ones I like." She teased him.

He tilted his head back on the wall paying no mind to her insane comment. Her words not stirring anything but more anger inside of him. The devil loved to use his tricks. He turned his head facing the direction of the streets and could see the car's headlights going by through the cracks of the board. He closed his eyes and thanked God.

"See I can be a good girl." She rubbed her hand on his chest. "I told you you had nothing to worry about, didn't I? Now what are you going to do to repay me for my good deed tonight?" Her brown eyes were trying to cast her nasty spells, but it wasn't going to work on him.

Jason removed her hand, feeling like bugs were crawling on his skin out of repulsion from her touch. "I'm going to get you saved."

Chapter 3

Audrey threw her high heels in the corner of her cramped and messy living room along with the rest of her collection of shoes, and walked to her kitchen to find something to put in her famished stomach. She checked her fridge first discovering that it was empty besides a half jug of water, and then checked her cabinets sad to see that there wasn't much going on in those either.

Finding a cup of ramen noodles, the chicken flavor the only kind she ate, she opened it, put some water in it and cooked it in the microwave. It had been a long night and she had nothing to show for it. That dorky man had come and decided to make her have a miserable time. He didn't even give her so much as a "thank you" for her helping him to avoid getting arrested by the cops.

Lulu, her furry white cat came up next to her rubbing against her leg, crying for something to eat. She bent down and petted her on the head to calm her down. Lulu was a stray kitten she'd found over a year ago. She was an inside and outside cat, though Audrey very seldom let her out due to the neighborhood she lived in. The kids who stayed there were horrible, training themselves up to become future murderers. They'd find animals on the street and get pleasure torturing them for their entertainment. Once she saw a dead cat hanging from one of the neighborhood's light poles while the children pointed and sniggered about what they'd just done. Audrey wanted to beat their little behinds.

The microwave rang notifying her that her noodles were done.

"I'm sorry Lulu. I'm having a hard time with money as of late. You and I are going to have share this for the time being."

She poured some in her kitty bowl and watched a little while as Lulu with haste started to eat away at her noodles. The possibility of having to give up Lulu brought her grief she didn't want to even think about, but having her around was taking more of her money. The vet visits coupled along with the food and litter expenses were beginning to become extra bills she couldn't afford. But without Lulu she'd be so lonely. Lulu came at a time in her life when it was her darkest hours. She was on the verge of committing suicide. However strange it may sound when Audrey found Lulu on the side of the streets, so small and fragile, with her eyes still closed whining for her mommy she discovered a reason to keep living beyond herself and her circumstances.

Something would just have to be done regarding her limited finances. Maybe she'd have to extend the hours she stayed on the corner, and by doing so gain more clients, giving her a boost in her stream of revenue.

It was too bad she had to lose a whole days' worth of salary due to that pestering dork. He'd left saying how he was going to get her saved or whatever. She hoped that didn't mean he was going to keep coming to bother her while she worked. If so, she'd just have to change corners, it's not like it gave her much luck tonight anyways.

What the man was preaching to her wasn't something she'd never heard before. Audrey already knew very well about God and Jesus. Growing up she used to attend church on frequent occasions with her mother. She didn't claim to be saved or anything though. Right now she didn't think God wanted much of anything to do with her.

Feeling exhausted she spread her body across her couch that was shabby and sinking in. Everything in her one bedroom apartment was falling apart or deteriorating; down from the sofa to the paint peeling off of the walls. But at least she had a place to rest her head. Life would get better. It's what Audrey had to keep telling herself to keep from relenting from the burdens of life.

Initially it going to be her day off from working the streets, Audrey forced her way to Lankford Avenue once again the night after. If she didn't make any cash tonight starvation might be the demise of her. There was nothing in her fridge and this morning she and Lulu had ate the last cup of ramen noodles together. Not having any family or emergency money to fall back on, tonight she would have to make some money by all means necessary.

Deciding to give it another chance she went to her lucky spot one more time. Scanning around the premises she found it to be empty, and the thing that was best of all was that she didn't see the dorky man anywhere to be found. Good, maybe she could buy a fridge full of grocery tomorrow. She couldn't remember the last time her fridge had a decent amount of food in it. Her stomach had gone seven hours without food today and was doing somersaults. If she were in the Olympics its performance would've won her a golden medal for sure.

Audrey leaned her head on the lamp post and lifted her hand to the dark sky.

"Hey there."

She almost leapt out of her skin not hearing anyone coming from behind her. She turned around with balled fist ready to defend herself if she had to. Although she maybe was skinny she could hold up a good fight.

The dorky man frowned at her. "Maybe you wouldn't have to be so jumpy if you got off of these streets."

Audrey gave out a dragged sigh. He was not about to ruin her night yet again.

"Ok. You said you wanted me to get saved right? Well, I don't want to be saved right now. So just leave me be. I'm trying to be as nice as I can to you right now, mister."

"Why don't you want to be saved?" Jason asked her bewildered. Who would desire to live a life like this out on the streets versus accepting Jesus?

"I just don't, OK."

"Well, what about you coming to my church. Then I ca—."

In the middle of his sentence a purple low rider with hydraulics rode up blazing loud rap music with curse words from a to z, creating a barbaric scene. The guy behind the wheel appeared to be more dangerous than the one from last night. He was husky like a body builder, his muscled arms were the size of tree logs, and he had heavy gold chains dangling around his neck. He also had tattoos all over his neck and body, mirroring your average thug.

"Hey lil mama, are you serving anyone tonight?" His arm hung out the car window as he attempted to show off even greater by making his car hop up and down to the beat of the music. When he spoke, he revealed a row of flashing gold teeth at the bottom of his mouth.

"Why yes, I am suga." She said getting down to business. "I start at fifty dollars." She began walking to the man's car more than ready to depart from the dorky man's presence.

"Wait." Jason inadvertently moved in her way, becoming a human blockade, making it impassable to go near the thug's car.

"What's your problem? Get out of my way." She tried walking around him, but he kept managing to move one pace ahead of her, successfully predicting her every steps.

"Is there something wrong here?" The man from the car

intervened. "Because if there is I can handle it for you lil mama." The man pulled his arm inside of his car and threateningly reached for his glove department.

"No." Audrey shouted not wanting anyone to get hurt. The only thing she had halfway considered a weapon was a small can of pepper spray tucked away inside of her purse. But that wouldn't do much good up against a gun. "There's nothing wrong, suga. I just need to speak with this mister for a moment."

She turned her attention to the dorky man and began talking loud enough only for his ears to hear her. "If you want to stay alive you need to get off these streets with your preaching and go somewhere else. It's dangerous out here."

"That's the exact reason why I'm trying to help you. So you can experience something better than this."

She searched the man's eyes. He seemed very adamant about getting her saved, but she didn't trust him, knowing there could be something else up his sleeves. Nowadays people didn't want to just help you simply to help. Audrey had to depend on herself to survive.

"Well, I'm sorry, but I have bills to pay, and unless you want to pay them for me I'm about to get back to work. I hope you find yourself another young lady out here to help."

Jason had waited at this spot for her for almost an hour, and before coming to this corner to wait for her Jason had saw no other girls like the last time. It must've been God wanting him to reach this lady in particular for some reason or another. If he could simply win this woeful sinner over he would get the executive pastor position for sure. All he needed was a few minutes alone with her, with no interruptions, and then he'd be able to talk her into changing her life around and going to Pastor James giving him the credit for it. Then he would have proved to him he could reach people.

"I'll pay you quadruple that." Jason said.

Audrey managed to keep her mouth from falling open. After preaching down so hard to her regarding her line of work he was going to pay for her services? But then again men were all weak when it came to sexual temptation. What made her think he would be any different?

"First you have to show me the money." Two hundred dollars were better than fifty, but she wasn't no fool.

He took out his wallet and showed her the crisp two hundred dollar bills.

The enchantress's eyes lit up with her love of money. She then walked over to the man in the car telling him that she wouldn't be serving him tonight. After he drove away she returned back to him, a tantalizing grin on her face. Suddenly there was a sinking feeling in his gut. Her smile and eyes were bewitching.

"You lead the way tonight, suga." she smirked. "Take me to your car, we can do whatever you want to there."

They arrived to his 2013 Lexus GS that was parked in an isolated area a block away behind an abandoned building. From the way he dressed so dorky and plain she wasn't expecting to discover that he cruised around in such a luxurious ride. The car was dark gray and shiny, looking brand new like it was fresh off of the car lot, and the windows were a deep black tint. He unlocked his car doors and they got inside.

The inside of his car was just as nice as the outside being spick-and-span. The interior was jet black and sleek with brown leather comfy seats. His car was imbrued with the scent of warm vanilla. This might've been the most clean and expensive car she'd ever been inside, actually she was sure that it was. She'd been in some unimaginable cars before.

Jason rubbed his perspiring hands on his dress pants. It's not like he was attracted to her or anything, but she made him feel uncomfortable to be around. The way she seductively gazed at him and her every movement was an attempt to get him to fall into sin—something he wasn't going to permit to happen. She was the devil's puppet and he wasn't about to get tangled into her strings of deceit.

Audrey looked over at him. Dorky man appeared to be nervous, like he was going to become sick.

"This will be over before you know it." She said with the aim at loosening him up a little, he wasn't about to faint on her watch. "Just tell me what you'd like."

The irritation he felt multiplied with every word that proceeded from her full lips. He grappled to remember what he wanted to tell her in order to convince her before she said anything else, but his mind failed him, drawing up a blank.

"I can do anything you want me to do." she rubbed her finger across her bottom lip. "I can make your legs tingle, your eyes roll to the back of your head in pleasure, and your lips quiver. Anything you want I can do." She said in a whispered racy voice. "I already have a condom so you don't have to worry about that." She pulled one from out of her purse.

Everything in him went numb. Jason couldn't believe what his eyes were seeing and what his ears were hearing. He'd never heard someone talk so provocative like she did.

She stretched her hand out to stroke him on his face.

"Don't touch me." He sprang away from her.

His body was pressed against the driver's door as if she was the plague. The pungent recoil he gave her causing her to feel like the dirtiest of trash.

"I'm not a monster." She looked out the window sadly.

"Well, why are you behaving like one?" Jason retorted, at the same time trying to calm his rapidly beating heart.

"You think I chose this life, huh?" Audrey felt herself getting angry now. "You don't know me or what I've been through. So stop looking from the outside in."

"Like I've told you before let me help you. I can help you to get out of this way of living."

Enragement about to take hold of her, Audrey closed her eyes in an effort to stop them from moistening. She wasn't about to allow this jerk to get her all emotional. "You can help me?" She let out a mad chuckle. "That's what all you men ever say. You all pretend you can be someone's knight in shining armor, or someone's road to freedom, only to really turn out to be just another prison."

Her stomach began to ache from lack of nourishment. She

abstained from clutching it, hoping that dorky man didn't hear it so he could have something else in addition to pick on her about.

Jason was sure he'd heard the sounds of her stomach. Her contorted face gave it away that she was in discomfort. "Are you hungry? Let me take you out to eat and tell you about my church."

"No, the more time I spend with you the more money I lose, and the more aggravated I become." She gathered up her things feeling stupid for falling to his ploy. He only wanted to bring her to his car to speak down on her more.

Jason could see that whatever he said to her, it wasn't going to get her to stay.

"Ok, well at least take these two hundred dollars. I told you I'd pay you and I meant my word." He pulled out his wallet. Since talking to her didn't do any good to convince her maybe money would. "And here, take my business card as well. Contact me if you ever need any help."

She didn't want to take his money, but she took it anyways along with his business card—*a girl's gotta eat right?* It was the least he could do for all of the troubles he'd caused her, though it was a fat chance she'd be reaching out to call him. If she did decide to go to church ever again, whichever one he attended she would do well to steer clear from.

Chapter 4

Pastor James approached Jason after church service was over in the hallway, gripping his hand firm in his as he gave him a handshake. His beady eyes were fixated intently on his. "I hope you seriously have pondered on and took into account all of the things of which we spoke about during our previous meeting."

"Yes sir, I did." Jason nodded.

"Good. Because the time is drawing nearer at the end of the year when the church leadership board will be coming together to discuss who will become our first executive pastor, and that's no small shoes to fill my boy."

"Yes sir, I understand."

Pastor James stood up straighter before walking off and went on to the next person in the hallway a few feet away. Instead of hounding him for questions and talking forwardly to him like he just did to Jason, he softened his demeanor. He even went as far as to flashing him a smile as he shook the young man's hand. Though it was small smile, it was still a smile nonetheless.

The man's hand that he was shaking name was David, and he was also Jason's older brother by two years. Everyone in the church loved David and his wife Cindy. Cindy was twenty-seven, the same age as Jason. Let everyone tell it Cindy and David were a match made in the heavens. Like Jason, both David and his wife were raised up in the church. They were a couple who were admired by all and they loved to share with anyone who'd listen about their testimony of how they remained pure until after marrying. Two months following their marriage they had got up in front of the church and told everyone about it, how God helped them to stay undefiled. Following their testimony in front of the church not long ensuing were they offered positions to become marriage pastors, and of course they accepted it. Jason was practicing purity too and probably living more righteous than David was. Where was his pat on the back, or job promotion? But this was a normal experience for Jason, since growing up he would always see the praises going to David, while he was the one being overlooked. At every chance he could get David would share of his noble deeds and all the good things that he'd done. And he also never failed to butter-up to Pastor James at every opportunity, and oh you better believe he was doing just that now.

David nodded his head just cheesing away as Pastor James spoke to him, like he was telling him the most interesting and funniest things his ears had ever heard before. Jason knew without uncertainty one of those people Pastor James was talking about who'd referred to him as being "unfriendly"—and whatever else he'd said—was David. There was no doubt in Jason's mind David wanted the executive pastor position for his grabbing, taking into account he was very active in the church and liked to move up the ladder as well. Everybody gravitated to him and his effortless charm and appeal. He was handsome, had a beautiful wife, it seemed like he had everything going for himself.

Not wanting to look at the scene any longer Jason turned on his heels to check on his ministry duties he had to complete before leaving to go home. He only took a few steps before he felt an arm come around his shoulders.

"Hey, bro. I was hoping I'd catch you before leaving church today." David gave his arm a squeeze.

Great, just the person he'd wanted to avoid for the rest of the day.

David was skilled on how to play multiple fields and act like he was really concerned about other people's lives and wellbeing. That was his way of winning people over, but Jason wasn't falling for his deceptive charm.

"Yeah, what for?" Jason removed his arm away.

"Cindy and I wanted to invite you over for dinner Friday night." David smiled over at him in such a manner, expecting for him to respond with excitement about his invite.

As if that was going to happen, the only reason he could want him over was so he could rub his happy married life in Jason's face, and to boast the more about them expecting their first baby that they were due to have in the next seven months. Whenever he got something new David was delighted to show off about it.

"No thanks." He mumbled.

"Why not?" David said dejected, more than likely let down due to the fact he couldn't get another person to brag about his successes to. "I can't remember the last time you even came over to our house to visit."

"I'm just busy is all, maybe some other time?" He walked away before David could annoy him any longer about it.

On his way driving home Jason thought about what had happened three nights ago inside of his car, thinking about the enchantress's advances alone made him clutch his steering wheel firmer in queasiness. She lived in a whole different world than what he'd ever known before. The reality that people chose to live that kind of disgraceful way was mind-boggling to him. The enchantress claimed she didn't choose that lifestyle, but that was only an excuse for her to cling to. As far as Jason was concerned people all have a choice for their behavior. They could decide whether to live a decent, upstanding life, such as himself, or not to. There were plenty of opportunities available on the job market, which was more acceptable than selling one's body on the streets.

Briefly checking his cell phone he found there to be no missed or unknown calls. He wondered if she was ever going to call him. He'd taken the precious time out of his hectic schedule in the middle of the night, two nights in a row, to go and show her kindness and she still hadn't reached out yet, or even given him a simple "thanks". Making a trip to Lankford Avenue was out of the question tonight. He had too many deadlines approaching on his church projects that he needed to close out on as soon as possible. Hopefully the enchantress would get some sense in her head and decide to get her life together.

Removing the thin white envelop from her PO Box she knew exactly what was inside of it before even having to reveal its contents. She tore it open and glossed her eyes over the paper reports that she'd received sent from the clinic, and then relaxed after reading everything turned out to be okay. After cheerfully folding them up she put them inside of her purse feeling like a weight had been lifted from off of her shoulders. But this alleviating moment would only last briefly until it would be time for her next checkup. The nervousness of waiting on tooth and nails for the results would soon return. Every time she went to get her monthly checkup she knew there could be a chance of getting bad news she didn't want to hear. With every one of her clients she'd always took safety precautions, and she never did anything without protection, but she could never be too sure in such a line of field.

When she entered into the business on Lankford Avenue, Audrey was introduced to a whole new environment she was unfamiliar with. There was this veteran who schooled her on how to handle the plights of the street life. She taught her the majority of what she knew today when it came to life on Lankford Avenue; how to avoid cops, how to not get robbed and how to stay alive in general. The woman's name was Alicia Beatty who was forty-seven years old and went by the alias name of Mama B. She'd been on the streets for over twenty-three years herself, claiming it was the only way she could support her three children. Their father had divorced her and up and left them without any money. According to Mama B it wasn't the white picket fence life she'd planned.

She'd try over and over to warn Audrey to leave the field when she ran into her at the age of seventeen on the streets nine years ago. "Go home honey. These streets ain't for you." The older woman kept telling her.

She also encouraged her that there was something better to life—Audrey was still trying to figure out what *better* Mama B was referring to. Audrey didn't listen to her warnings of course, because she had no one to depend on like most people her age did. She was all alone and by that young age of seventeen she was already growing accustomed on having to take care of herself. As time passed she didn't see Mama B on the streets anymore, Audrey never knew what happened to her but she always remembered her advice. Maybe she had finally found her way out like she'd wanted to for so long. If that was the case then that was good for her. Hopefully one day she could follow suit and get out of the life of prostituting as well, for so long it'd been the only life that Audrey knew.

Keeping the care alive, Audrey returned the same concerned spirit that Mama B showed to her whenever she would see a young girl on Lankford Avenue, by forewarning them to go back home, (supposing that they had one), while they still had the chance to do so. If they didn't take heed to her supplications—which none of them ever did, she would then give them advice on how to at least stay safe while roaming the streets.

She saw girls as young as thirteen years of age before working on the corners. Though it was always unbelievable for her to witness, sadly it was beginning to become a normal thing to see. The reason most minors were out prostituting was because of their pimps, who fed them lies about them being together if they did what they were told, or some were threatened into submission. That's why Audrey now rode solo. Pimps didn't care about the age of the girls that they use. It was all about whether or not if they can make a buck out of them. And to make matters worse the perverted men who rode through the streets looking for a quick fix to satisfy their craving flesh didn't care either. She'd been a minor before on the streets. When she was fifteen she told a man her age before, all he did was smile in her face, said that it didn't matter and that he would be willing to pay even more for whatever she did.

Audrey took a bus down to Baskerville's road to see Trina, the only person she could consider somewhat of a friend. Trina was also a prostitute. She'd met her around five years back when this man tried to pick pocket her. Audrey gave her a helping hand and they both jumped the guy. Luckily he didn't have any weapons on him; those were Audrey's more amateur days. She knew better now before intervening into a fight, to check them first to see if it looked like they had any outline of a weapon in their pockets. The world was becoming crazier by the day so now most of the time Audrey stayed in her own lane, which was the best thing for her to do if she wanted to live.

Ever since that night she'd helped Trina out they'd become associates, having each other's back and watching out for one another. Lately Trina had been missing in action, becoming worried Audrey felt the need to go and check up on her today. Trina had a real nasty drug addiction since she'd known her. She urged her to quit, but once a person was strung out on cocaine and other highly addictive drugs it was hard to kick the habit.

"Promise me you'll never try drugs Audrey." Trina cried to her one day, shaking from the withdrawals she was having from cocaine. She'd tried everything from drug rehab to flushing all of her drugs down the toilet, but somehow Trina would always manage to get her hands on more drugs and relapse, but Audrey never wanted to give up on her, being hopeful there could be a way to save her.

Knocking on her door, Audrey kept glancing over her shoulder's every few seconds making sure that no one was running up on her. The neighborhood was always on the news for something or another. It was a common place for crack heads and drug user's; a few reasons why she never visited Trina at the daunting hours of the night. It had to be broad daylight. Even then you had to safeguard yourself, some robbers didn't care what time of the day they could get you, what mattered is that they got you.

After knocking on the door for some time Trina opened her door with dark circles underneath her eyes and untamed hair. Her appearance was horrid.

"Hey, what you doing here girl?" She patted her hair down completely out of it. Her pupils were dilated, coincided with a runny nose.

"I came here to check up on you. I was worried, I haven't heard from you in a while." It was evident that Trina was high on drugs. Solace seized at Audrey's heart as she noticed Trina's sharp collar bone protruding from her robe. Her body was shriveling away.

"I'm aight." she closed her tattered robe and looked behind her shoulder. "But right now ain't a good time, though."

Understanding what she meant Audrey slowly shook her head. There must've been a man in her house she was shooting up some dope with, exchanging sex for drugs. She hung her head low knowing she couldn't do or say anything about it to try and stop her. Trina wasn't going to hear it—she wasn't hearing it for the past five years that they'd known each other.

"Ok Trina." She gave in reluctantly. "Just be safe, ok girl."

Trina nodded her head, smiling facetiously.

"Oh, wait." Trina said before she turned to walk away. "There was this guy one day, not too long ago at the corner looking for you."

"Was he a regular customer or something?" It wasn't unusual for regular's to ask for their favorites.

"Nah, I ain't never seen him before. But He knew your government name and everything." Trina said energetically.

Becoming a little concerned Audrey meditated on who it could be. She'd never let a customer know her true name before. And aside from Trina there were only a few other people she disclosed her real name too, she could count those people on one hand. Who could this person be that was looking for her?

"Do you remember what he looked like?"

As she tried to conjure up an image Trina squint her eyes in concentration. "He was tall, black, and skinny, with a short fade."

Well that wasn't going to help her out at all, Trina had just described about one third of Audrey's clients.

"Do you remember anything else? Anything that sticks out?" She investigated for more answers that could aid her in identifying the nameless man.

"Oh yeah." Trina snapped her fingers. "He had tattoos of two wings on his neck, one on each side."

Audrey's heart hammered turbulently as her knee's buckled. She knew exactly who Trina was talking about. How did he find her? She was sure she had covered her tracks so he couldn't discover where she was.

"And he said that if I knew you to let you know that he was looking for you and that he was gonna find you." Trina smiled. "Looks like you gotta an admirer. Girl, he fine too, I would get with him. Heeeey!"

Audrey ignored her ignorance; all she needed to know was one vital thing. "You didn't tell him where I stayed, did you?"

"No." Trina said after pausing.

She didn't know if Trina was telling her the truth or not—it was Audrey's earnest hope she was telling her the truth. She left Trina's house that day trying to figure out what she was going to do to not run into him. The last thing she remembered about Cash, if that was even his real name, was his large hands squeezing tightly around her throat. He was her first and last pimp, the one who gave her the identity of Jade and told her that her only worth was prostituting, and he was the one she needed to avoid like a disease if she wanted to stay alive.

Out of the fear of possibly running into him on the streets, she stayed away from Lankford Avenue that night. At least in one area did the dorky man bring her good fortune. With the money he'd given her she was able to fill her fridge up and she was also able to buy Lulu some of her own cat food, all while still being able to have some spare change from it. Because she had some of that left over she wasn't too stressed about losing money for the night. Some time away would give her an opportunity to think about what she needed to do if she had to relocate. Moving around from city to city and state to state was a frequent thing for her as a child, but Tampa had become her home these past nine years. Plus she didn't have any money saved up to make a big move like that. It would be better for her to keep a low key for a few weeks, and maybe after his searching came up void he'd give up and scram. Hopefully chance would have it that way.

Chapter 5

It happened in the still hours of the night. At first she thought it was a nightmare, she had nightmares all of the time, but the intensifying banging noise woke her from out of her sleep letting her know it was real. She scrambled her hands around her dresser searching for something—anything, which she could use as a weapon and grabbed firmly onto her hair brush. It was better than nothing. The knocking on her apartment front door grew louder. She went to the front room and scooped Lulu into her arms. She meowed, squirming to get free, shaky from the ruckus.

Her mind was not working correctly for her at the moment. She didn't know who it could be at her door this time of hour, but the way they were knocking was not nice. Maybe it was the landlord looking for his last two months of overdue rent. Usually he would comply with her on a late payment plan, but since third month's rent was soon imminent, and she was so far behind, she suspected it could be him warning her he needed his rent money this time around. She was about to check to see if it was him through her peep hole until she heard his menacing voice, making her stop dead in her tracks. That voice she'd hoped she would never have to hear again during her lifetime.

"My beautiful Jade, open the door. I know you're in there." His voice was slow and brimming with taunt.

Audrey clutched Lulu closer to her chest, and gripped the brush tighter in her hand. The voice coming from the other end of the door was Cash. She would've called the police, but she didn't pay her cell phone bill last week. The only thing she could do now was hope he'd go away after thinking nobody was home. She covered Lulu's mouth to prevent her from making any more noises.

He stopped bamming on the door. The thick of the night made her feel even more nervous, she couldn't see if he had left or not. She stood as motionless as she could as the silence surrounded her.

"Jade! I said open the door!" he pulled violently at her door knob. "You think I was going to let you play me for some kind of a sucka!"

She covered her mouth to keep herself from screaming, but it was obvious he already knew she was inside and that he was going to find his way in at all cost.

Wanting to live to see another day Audrey thought fast and

secured Lulu inside of her pet cage. She then hurriedly ran to her room, threw on some jeans and tank top from her dirty hamper and began throwing as much clothes as she could fit inside of her backpack. Her hands shook as she grabbed the first things that her eyes could see in the dark.

As she ran to her bathroom to grab her toothbrush and some accessories she heard Cash say, "It was easy to find you too. What did I tell you about trusting these dope heads out on the streets? All I had to do was give her some drugs and she spilled where you lived at."

Gritting her teeth in anger, at herself mostly, Audrey began to pace herself faster so she could escape through the window of her bedroom. She should've known to be extra cautious with whatever information she gave Trina concerning her. Her being too quick to trust people sometimes, she thought maybe she'd made a new friend. But addicted people would do anything just for a hit.

Her backpack wasn't but so big so she was done putting as much as she could stuff inside of it, including her purse. She grabbed the pet carrier Lulu was inside and lowered her out of the window first.

Lulu started making more whining sounds again. "Shhhh Lulu, be quiet." Petrified Cash had heard and was coming to the back to kill her she paused trembling.

Luckily he was still making a commotion at her front door. Audrey knew already her neighbors wouldn't bother to help her in the kind of apartment complex she lived at. They were scared of being shot or killed themselves. Even if she could call the cops, they wouldn't help her much either or keep her out of harm's way, they disregarded the neighborhood enough as it is. The authorities couldn't promise her she'd be protected.

She gently threw her backpack out and held her breath in as she slid her way out of the small window. As soon as her feet hit the grass she grabbed the cage Lulu was in, slung her backpack over her shoulders and ran. She ran as fast as she could not knowing where she was going. All she knew was that she had to flee as far away from Cash as her feet could take her.

She ran through the roads for what seemed like hours. Time had escaped her. When she got as far away as to where her apartment complex was long gone and no longer in sight she bent over heaving for air. Her lungs felt like they were running on a treadmill. No matter how much she gasped for air her breathing wouldn't slow down. She fell on the dewed grass to the side of the secluded road in tears. What was she going to do now? She had nowhere to go and nobody to turn to. Two or three cars passed her on the opposite lane, but they didn't inconvenience themselves to stop.

Audrey didn't know why she was so surprised to find herself in such a predicament. She should be accustomed to this kind of reckless life, a life that would never get any better for her, only worse. She was destined to be miserable for the rest of her life. It was like whenever things finally seemed like they were going decent, that's when something bad would happen. Ever since she was a little girl it was always this way. One thing she could be certain about was that her life was headed nowhere, but she deserved it. It's not like she brought much good to society by being a tool to assist men to commit every kind of evil act. She was no doubt getting punished for her all of her wrong deeds, which was well merited.

The thought of going to a shelter crossed her mind, but many didn't accept pets. Separating from Lulu was out of the question. Having Lulu around was what helped Audrey to get through her rough patches. Lulu was a big part of what kept her to keep going. Knowing sulking around wouldn't solve any of her problems she stood up and brushed herself off. After picking up Lulu and what belongings she had left she walked further down the dark road, towering trees on every side of her. She picked up speed, fearing what wild beast may be lurking in the ominous trees to come and tear her to pieces.

It was no way she was planning to return back to her apartment and risk getting caught by Cash, that would be like going to meet her death. Audrey didn't want to die just yet. She at least wanted to get her life cleaned up to have something half decent to leave behind when her life was all said and done. Being a deplorable prostitute wasn't what she wanted to be remembered as after her death; that was if anyone even cared to remember her when she was dead and gone.

A wandering lost soul having no place in life was what she felt like. Just going wherever her body would take her. Her legs began to sway, weakening with every step she took. Lulu was hollering more and her stomach was now telling her that it was hungry.

About a yard or so down she spotted some fast food joints on a well-lit street. It was late in the night so nobody was really out, save for some semi-truck drivers making their quick stops before winding down or heading back on the road for the night. A few of them glanced at her in her deranged state as she drug all of her belongings to a table. Sitting Lulu's cage beside her she sat down exhausted and confused on what to do or where to go next.

One of the restaurant servers came up to her with an air of concern. "Are you ok miss?" The stocky lady in her thirties asked her.

"Yes." Audrey nodded and attempted to smile at the lady.

"Let me know if there's anything I can do for you ok." The lady left her and went back to wiping some empty tables.

"It's ok Lulu, I'm going to get us out of this somehow." Her little fury paws shimmied through a small opening of the cage, wanting to be let out. Lulu hated being in her pet carrier, she'd always had a problem out of her whenever Audrey had to take her to the vet.

Scavenging through her purse she searched for the left over money she still had from the dorky man. She found the money as well as his business card. For the first time she paid attention to it and scanned it over, flipping it through her fingers.

So dorky man's name was Jason Goodman.

Inscribed below his name on the card were his business and cell phone number. Her mind lingered for a moment. She shook her head. No this guy wouldn't help her and she couldn't trust him. But then again she had nowhere else to go. She couldn't stay at this fast food joint forever. It was worth a try.

She found the stocky lady a table down. "Matter of fact there is something you can do for me. Do you have a phone that I could use?"

Jason was in a paradisiacal sleep when the ring of his cell phone roused him. No one ever called him this late in the night before. *Had somebody lost their minds?* It had better been an emergency. While still lying in his bed he checked his phone to see it was from an unknown caller. Surely this couldn't be the enchantress calling him at all times of the night.

"Hello." He answered, nettled to be woken up out of his slumber.

"Sorry for waking you." From the sound of her voice he knew it was her; the enchantress. So money did talk for her after all. "I wanted to know if you'd still like to help me, like you said you would."

This was unbelievable. Had she called just to ask him this, this late in the hour? "Yes. Is that all you called to ask me?" Jason closed his eyes, he was ready to go back to sleep.

"No." she paused. "I'm in need of your help, and I'm in need of it right now. Could you meet me? It's an emergency." He picked up a hint of desperation sheathing in her tone.

Jason glanced over at his alarm clock set atop his night stand; it read two twelve am.

With grumbling he removed his covers from off of him and labored to get out of his warm bed. "Where are you?" He knew God could not ignore to reward him for this great sacrifice.

He arrived to the place the enchantress told him she'd be at. When he entered he saw her sitting at a table booth near the back, shaken up, with all of her possessions disorderly scattered around her. Next to her he noticed she had a cat being detained in a carrier. Jason loathed cats.

Spotting him come through the door of the restaurant she'd never been so happy to see him—flabbergasted he really even came. Maybe, just maybe, dorky man—she meant Jason Goodman, really did want to help her out of the goodness of his Christian heart.

He sat down across from her at the table, with a slight grimace. He did not want to be there. Whatever she required aid in relation to she needed to make it quick, so he could be in and out without delay. Upon him taking a seat a lady waiter placed in front of her a cup of steaming coffee.

She thanked the lady as a child would when they were in trouble and somebody had just bailed them out.

"No problem miss, let me know if you need anything else." The waiter shifted her attention to Jason. "I'm glad to see you have good people in your life to come to your side during times of trouble." She grinned at him before walking away.

Jason nodded in agreement at the ladies comment. He was after all doing such a noble deed. He was glad at least someone took notice.

"Hey." The enchantress smiled at him as if they were old friend's catching up over a lunch meal.

"So what's this all about?" Jason had no time for small talk.

"Well, I suppose if you want to get straight to the point." She fastened her hands around her cup of coffee appearing hesitant. "I need your help."

"That was already discussed over the phone. What kind of help do you need?"

He examined the clothes she was wearing. Even now, clothed in a snug fitting tank top, did she find it necessary to have to have her cleavage out and her skin exposed for everyone to see.

"First I have a question." She looked at him curiously. "If I receive help from you what is it you want from me? If it's not sex, then what?"

"Shhhh." He lifted his finger to his mouth, at the same time scanning around the restaurant. He didn't want anyone to have heard the disreputable word she'd just spoken. And he also didn't want anyone he knew to see him there with her, if they did it wouldn't do well with his reputation. No one was paying them any mind so that was a reprieve.

"Sorry." She shrugged. It was clear he did not like the word sex.

"All I'd like for you to do is come to my church and say how you've been changed thanks to my help. And that's it."

"That sounds simple enough." Audrey glanced sideways before continuing. "So…I'm suddenly out of a place to stay. If I agree to do that for you, could you let me stay with you? Only for a little while."

He looked at her like she'd gone bonkers. It was evident she had if she was serious about what she was asking of him, which she seemed to be. "Are you kidding? I don't even know your name to let alone allow you to stay inside of my house."

"Well you'd think a person who cared so much about someone's soul would've thought to ask for that person's name first."

Jason stared at her for a moment. "Well what's your name then?"

She debated on if she should tell him her real name or not.

"Audrey." She finally said. She didn't know why she had told him her real name. When was she going to learn? Well it didn't matter much now anyhow. Cash already knew she was in Tampa.

"Ok Audrey, my name's Jason if you didn't know by now. And I can help you, but I can't help you in that capacity."

"You have a wife at home or something?" She knew he was another dog masked behind his supposed good boy image.

"No. I'm not married. I stay alone." Jason's eyes fell.

From his concession, and the way his eyes drooped like a sad puppy that'd strayed away from its mommy, Audrey could tell he was despondent about the fact he wasn't married yet. She wondered why he wasn't already, but then she remembered his hard temperament. Yeah, he might be plain, but with a nice wardrobe change he'd be cute. His personality however, was another issue she didn't know could be fixed. So far he was not very flattering. If he was anything with the ladies like how he was with her then it was a no brainer why he was still single.

"I guess I won't be able to testify in front of your church for you then."

Jason leaned back in his chair wondering had he invested this much time and energy in her, all for it to go to waste. God had to lead him to her for a reason, right? But what she was asking of him was too ample of a task for him. He didn't want a woman, let alone a woman of her scandalizing stature, to be staying in his home.

"There has to be some other way that I can help you. At least let me take you to a shelter or something. Don't you have any family here I can drop you off to?"

"If I did do you think I would've called you?" She said sarcastically. "Forget it. I knew you wouldn't help me. You can just leave now, please."

"What?"

"I asked you to leave. I just don't want to waste anymore of your time. I'm sorry for calling you here so late in the night." Audrey shouldn't have felt so let down about it like she did, she'd already foreknown he wouldn't do it. And to be honest she couldn't too much blame him for saying no. She was pretty much a stranger to him. But still, she felt destitute about it. She'd tried though right? She would just have to think of something else—exactly what, she didn't know.

Jason stood up from the table to leave. It was a real pity all of his efforts were going down the drain like this. Pastor James's' confidence would have to be won over some other way.

The sounds of her sniffles made him come to a halt. He looked back at her. She was staring out of the window crying silently with her head lain down on her arm, looking abandoned and dismal. For some reason he started feeling sympathy towards her—but not enough to allow her into his home. Before going back to sleep tonight he'd just have to pray for her. He tried to take another step towards the direction of the exit, but couldn't. The weight of his feet became heavy, being too much for his legs to carry. Then those words came echoing in his ears like rolling thunder:

When was the last time you brought someone to Christ outside of this building or opened up your home to a stranger?

Never. He'd never opened up his home to a stranger, nor had he ever brought someone to Christ, even from the inside of his church. With his deep rooted desire to impress Pastor James Jason slowly walked back to her table as if an unknown force was maneuvering him. He knew he was probably about to make one of the biggest mistakes of his life.

"You can stay with me." He said through tight lips. "But only for a short time."

She wiped away tears as she looked up at him. "Thank you! Thank you!"

Audrey almost couldn't believe it—actually she couldn't believe it. Before he could begin to think to change his mind she grabbed up her things and followed him to his car. Knowing what it looked like already she even got there before he did.

Chapter 6

The neighborhood was for those of the upper class, she could tell by the extravagant homes they kept passing by. They were all built orderly with luxurious craftsmanship. The roads were smooth, like they'd been freshly coated with paint, and everybody's lawn was mowed. Palm trees were sprouted about creating a tropical utopia. Even in the dark of the night the neighborhood's grandeur could be recognized.

They pulled in the long driveway of a house so beautiful and wondrous, it could be featured in one of those home magazines. It was made of earth toned bricks, with Spanish tile roof shingles. The grass was cut so neat and leveled that Audrey could swear all of the strands of grass were of the same exact length. It was a grand one story home built of refined splendor.

"Dust your shoes off before coming inside please." Jason unlocked the front door wiping his feet on the welcome rug.

Audrey dusted hers off as well and then followed him inside. Lulu was scooting around in her cage behaving anxious to bet let out.

His house was spacious, tidy and elegant. In the main living room were black leather sofas, the décor was mostly neutral colors; gray and black, not surprisingly matching his character, but he had a lot of fancy artwork on many of the walls. They were philosophical and abstract. To be honest she didn't get the gist of them and what the paintings were trying to depict, but she guessed in order to appreciate their beauty you'd have to stare at them for a long time with your head slightly tilted to the side—well at least that's what she saw in some movie anyway.

There was also sliding glass doors in the living area open to a wraparound cabana and lanai. The large kitchen was delightful; it had black granite countertops and an island in the center, white cabinets and lots of shelf space, Audrey could just imagine all of the food that could fit inside of them. The dining room was adjacent to it. The focal of the space being a black rectangular table dressed with silver table runners. Every room in the house had high ceilings.

They entered a grand room in the house that had a tan oval rug at the foot of the queen bed. Adorned on the bed was a tan polyester comforter with matching pillow sets. A white dresser with a mirror was placed on the wall facing opposite of the bed. White flowing long curtains that touched the floor covered the windows in the room. Audrey felt like she was in a chateau. In all of her life she'd never been in a house so beautiful.

"This is the guest room, the room you'll be staying in for now."

"Thank you. I really do appreciate your help." And she really did, this was more generosity from him than what she was expecting.

"Yeah, well we'll talk more tomorrow regarding your living arrangements and our deal. I'm tired."

Audrey nodded.

Before he stepped out he turned back around with downward slant brows at Lulu's cage.

"And make sure you keep that thing confined please." He shut her door.

Audrey stood for a while in awe. She couldn't believe that she was in such a remarkable house. She bent down and released Lulu from her cage. Lulu ran out immediately, appreciative to be uncaged, and started sniffing around the place that was foreign to her. It would've been nice if he'd let her shower first, but oh well. She was just happy she'd found a place to stay for the time being. What happened next she would just have to work that out.

The smell of food that'd been cooking for too long hit his nostrils causing him to wake from his sleep the next morning. Quickly getting out of his bed his raced his way to the kitchen. Why he was so stupid to allow her in his house was beyond him. Now the woman was about to burn his house down to the ground.

Walking through the hallway her cat rushed towards him, peering up at him with its big blue eyes and pointy sharp whiskers that looked like they could jab him just by brushing against them. Didn't he tell her to keep this thing locked up?

"Shoo!" He moved his leg away as the creature tried to rub up against him. He was about to kick it away, but then he'd have to come into contact with it, which was something he didn't want to do. He was never allowed pets when he was younger and now he understood why. They were a nuisance. Not being able to have pets he didn't miss out on anything. Looking at the beast fur made him feel like flees were crawling in his hair. The hideous being confirmed his beliefs even more, animals weren't meant to live inside of people's houses. Their proper place was being out in the wild; their natural habitat. The creature looked up at him with its marble eyes.

He hurried and scampered past it. When he got to his kitchen he saw Audrey at the stove cooking. What little she had on caused him to have to turn his face away. The mini shorts she wore didn't cover up entirely what they were supposed to.

"What're you doing?"

Audrey turned around. Jason had one of his hands covering half of his face.

"I'm cooking. I wanted to show you my gratitude for you letting me stay here."

A hard gooey like object felt like it was stuck in his throat, he swallowed using his saliva to try to dissipate it. "You...you need to put on some clothes."

It was kind of comical for Audrey watching him stammering. It was apparent he hadn't been around females much. "Sure, but the little bit of stuff I have in my backpack is pretty much the same as what I'm wearing now."

She joined him at the dining table after changing into one of his long sleeved button up shirts and some khaki shorts he'd given her to wear.

"There, that's better." He told her.

"I don't think I will be able to go out like this." She rolled up the sleeves that extended past her hands.

"Of course not, but while you're around me you need to dress appropriately. I guess I can take you to get some more clothes later next week. For now you need to wear what I have to give you at the moment."

"I don't have that kind of money to buy a new set of clothes."

"I'll pay for it."

What? Was she hearing him correctly? "Are you serious? All of this for a testimony?"

He shook his head. "It's more than just about the testimony, but you don't have to concern yourself about that part."

Audrey wondered what he meant by that. His eyes became unfocused as if he were thinking about something else.

Jason had to analyze a way to keep his neighbors from being suspicious and from improper rumors being started. It was a tight knit community, so everyone knew each other. If they started seeing him coming in and out of his house with a woman who sprang up from out of nowhere they might start thinking absurd thoughts about he and Audrey's affiliation with one another. To add onto the matter having the opposite sex live in his house with him without being married to her first was something his faith frowned upon. Although he was only providing her a place to stay to help her he still wanted to keep himself right with God and in the public eye, and for there not to be any indication of the appearance of evil going on. "While you're staying here if any of my neighbors ask you our relationship with one another just tell them you're my long lost sister ok?"

"Isn't it a sin for a Christian to lie?"

"You're going to be the one lying so it shouldn't be much of a big deal for you. It can just add on to the heap of mounting sins you already have, and not to mention the disciple crimes you commit."

"I'm not a criminal you know." Audrey frowned.

"I don't know where you think you live but as of now prostitution is illegal in the State of Florida. As a matter of fact it's illegal in all fifty states of the US so that makes you a criminal."

Audrey wanted to give him a piece of her mind, but instead she scraped a forkful of her eggs allowing his comment to fly over her head. She was after all staying in the man's house and didn't want to say anything that could risk her being thrown out. Audrey noticed he wasn't eating any of his food.

"Why aren't you touching your food? Are you scared I have some sort of disease and that you might become infected or something?

I'm STD free. I can even show you the papers to prove it."

Jason didn't oppose her offer. She went to retrieve the papers from her purse and then showed them to him. Jason looked over them carefully.

"That's good to know." Jason looked down at the food she'd attempted to cook. "Though I was more concerned with how it taste. It doesn't look too appetizing." Everything on his plate was burnt.

"It tastes good to me." Audrey replied defensively.

Jason pushed away his serving. "Suit yourself then."

"Well fine, I'll just eat yours as well." She grabbed his plate and set it beside hers. "It doesn't do any good to waste food." He might be used to splurging and throwing away money, but one thing Audrey wasn't was wasteful. To be able to afford such a comfortable living, he must've brought in a hefty income.

"Where do you work at anyways?" She asked him.

"I work at my church as a minister."

"You can really get paid working at a church and live like this?"

"Yes and I'm about to head there now for a meeting. Until you have cleaned up decently you will stay inside. I don't want any of my neighbors to see you in this state. Don't leave to go out anywhere. Don't touch anything, and don't go in my room."

The longer the meeting dragged the antsier he became—and the more his leg convulsed underneath the table with a mind of its own. A complete stranger was at his home who could vandalize and steal anything of her liking. She could let God knows who in his house while they wreaked havoc doing the devil's business. He could imagine her now laughing as she and her buddies rode off with a load full of his valuable possessions in their car, on their way to pawn it all. Really, what was Jason thinking? Why would he allow her to stay at his house all by herself and give her the freedom to possibly steal his things? *Why!?* In the middle of asking himself why someone tapped him on his shoulder.

"Jason, Mr. Thomson's asking you a question." Justin whispered over to him.

Jason sat up straighter in his chair and forced his leg to stop shaking. Justin Watson was somewhat of like a duteous pupil to him. He was eight years his junior and came under Jason's wing to receive counsel about leadership lessons. Justin told him one day the reason why he'd chosen Jason to be his mentor was because he noticed how Jason was mature, had everything together and he liked how Jason ran his ministries with expertise and efficiency; the kid was smart and knew what he was talking about. He was a children's Bible study teacher for the youth ministry, one of the three ministries that Jason was over. Despite his budding age of only being nineteen, he was a young man who was eager to learn and he had his head on straight, which was a rare thing for his headed for nowhere generation.

"Jason, did you hear what I just said?" Mr. Thomson asked him with a sly look on his face.

Mr. Thomson had been serving in the church since Jason was in his diapers. Since he'd served for so long he thought he deserved seniority and for people to bow down to him, always holding his head held high.

"No sir, my apologies. My mind was temporarily off somewhere else."

"Concerning the seriousness of the matter don't you think your mind ought to be here with us, discussing the issue at hand?" Gordon Thomson, his son—and puppet—chimed in.

Both of them looked the same, having wide noses and inward sloped foreheads putting Jason in the mind of sharks whenever he saw them. And bloodthirsty sharks they were, seizing every opening they could utilize to dominate, using their conceitedness as a tactic to do so. Jason was aware that Mr. Thomson thought he deserved the executive pastor position. He had served longer than Jason, was older and much wiser than Jason, and he knew the ends and outs of the ministry more than Jason; it was only fair that the position go to him right? The way Mr. Thomson was cutting him with his dark piercing eyes told Jason he was thinking those very thoughts.

Jason clasped his hands together in front of him on the table, remaining composed. They weren't going to provoke him like the way they were attempting to do so. "I agree this is a serious matter. Please repeat yourself so I can give you my undivided attention."

Mr. Thomson shook his head with discontent. "I asked you, being the head over the youth ministry, what do you think we should do regarding Paul Jr. hitting another child in the face during children's church."

"I think he should be kicked out of children's church for his misbehavior, indefinitely. Let him have church with the adults now so he can get his act together. He can use some growing up."

"We don't just give up on people Jason. Of course the proper punishment will be administered, but don't you think that's being a bit too much kicking him out indefinitely? A child flourishes much better when their surround by their peers."

Jason could tell Mr. Thomson couldn't give a hoot one way or the other if the boy was kicked out or not. His central goal was to show up Jason in front of everybody in the meeting and in turn win them over on his side. The meeting consisted of him, Justin, the Thomson's, the youth pastor, and three other youth teachers who were there when the incident occurred.

Mr. Thomson continued before giving Jason the opportunity to reply. "You see the central ambition of Waters of Life ministry is reaching the people." He sneered.

Jason felt himself stirring inside. Mr. Thomson was strategically throwing his bait to trap and make a fool out of him. His words echoed those of Pastor James. Yes indeed, Mr. Thomson knew the ins and outs of the church well and how to play politics, but Jason had something up his sleeves too.

"I agree. Reaching the people is top priority, but providing them safety here is as well. What message does that show to the other children when we allow them to misbehave by simply giving them a small slap on the wrist?"

"God is a God of forgiving, is he not? And as His people we should be a reflection of Him and all that He stands for, am I right?"

Mr. Thomson glanced around the room waiting for people to bob their head in approval—and they did! Justin was the only one who didn't, though his expression showed he wanted to. Jason felt himself losing ground to Mr. Thomson, and fast.

"Well God is also a God of wrath and judgment, but people don't like to see that side of Him though."

"If I do say so myself I don't think you'd like to see that side of Him either. If we're all honest here, without His mercy and love every single one of us would be headed straight for hell. Wasn't it His love after all that sent Jesus on the cross to bear our sins, to cleanse us of all of our unrighteousness?"

The nods and "amen's" articulated from everyone around the table told Jason he'd been overridden.

"That being said I believe we should give the boy one more chance as we monitor his behavior. It is then that if he keeps acting up we will have to make other arrangements. All of those in favor say I."

The vote was unanimous, his own pupil even betrayed him by voicing *"I"* in approval to Mr. Thomson's suggestion. Jason left the meeting feeling humiliated and stomped on. Who did Mr. Thomson think he was? Just because he was there for longer didn't make him more qualified. Jason worked hard too and sacrificed for God. He didn't act like most people his age by going to the clubs, drinking or fornicating. When was the Lord going to bless Him for His good doing and obedience? No instead he had a detestable prostitute at as his home doing Lord knows what. He was so wrapped up in his rage that he didn't know anyone was in front of him in the hallway until he bumped right into them. Annoyed he was about to tell them to watch where they were going, but when he looked up into her soft face he couldn't help but to keep his frustrations held in.

Cindy smiled at him. "Hey brother in law, I haven't seen you in ages."

Jason looked sideways. Her shiny brown hair swept just above her shoulders, she was elegant and modest. Her chocolate skin was glowing. She was so beautiful.

"I've been busy." He said plainly.

"That's what you always say." She laughed, but the disappointment in her voice was audible. "Ever since David and I got married I haven't seen or heard from you much. We used to hang out all the time when we were younger."

"That was then, this is now." That's what he wanted to tell her, but instead Jason remained quiet.

The silence became awkward. Cindy played with her dangling earring in her left ear.

"By the way you never told me congratulations." She placed her hand on her bloated belly.

So she was a like David after all—wanting praises. Maybe that's why she'd chosen him.

"Congratulations." He mumbled. "Well I have to go."

Cindy opened her mouth like she wanted to say something else, but stopped.

"Alright, I'll see you later then." She waved

Chapter 7

Audrey lay floating in the tranquilizing underground pool, listening to the wind as it whistled melodiously through the palm trees. She couldn't resist herself when Jason had left. She'd been eyeing the pool ever since she'd stepped foot in his house and discovered he had one. A quick swim before he came home wouldn't do any harm. She'd sneak back in before he made it home. Just ten minutes more and she'd get out.

It was so peaceful here. Audrey couldn't remember the last time she'd felt this way; the feeling of being still and giving her mind an escape from worry, from life. Just yesterday she was in her confined little apart, but now she was in a place that could fit three of her living rooms in just one of its bathrooms. This wasn't going to last forever—that she knew, but just for a moment did she want to take it all in before it was time for her to go back to her shameful life again on Lankford Avenue.

Once Cash saw she'd fled from her apartment and couldn't find her then he would have no other choice but to go back to where he came. Cash was not a man to waste time so she felt confident he wouldn't keep searching for her for too long. He once told her before sending her out on the streets one night that time was money and that she'd better get in as many guys in one night as she could or he'd beat her until she lost consciousness. She shook her head hoping it would make the memories go away. For ten years she'd lived as though she'd had amnesia, erasing every morsel of memory in her brain that had anything to do with Cash and her painful childhood. Doing this made it less despairing for her to live.

She climbed out of the pool and headed in before Jason returned home. She reached her hand to open the slide door, but it slid open without her touching it. She looked up. Jason had opened it and he was looking furious.

"What are you doing? I told you not to touch anything or to go outside." Jason kept his eyes from her body, which was clothed with only her bra and underwear.

Although he wasn't friendly to begin with, she could see there was something different about him. Something must've happened at his church meeting to get him all bothered, but he didn't have to take it out on her.

"I only went out for a swim. Besides your pool area is screened in so no one saw me."

"I don't care. You don't need to be parading your body out in my house like this." Why was this lady so immodest and immoral? Why couldn't she be more like Cindy, who was modest and pure? The childish smile she had on her face made him the more enraged. She was obviously getting a laugh out of the frustrations she was bringing upon him. The woman was a devil, wanting to prick and prick at him until he gave in into her vices.

"Why? I'll let you have a go with me since you've been being so nice. Don't be shy, I know that's what you've probably been itching for all along. You beginning to like what you see, aren't you?" She said in a sultry voice while rubbing her index finger across her chest.

"No! No I'm not beginning to like what I see! In fact I'm repulsed! Is that all you know how to do is to be a dirt cheap whore!?"

Smack!

Before Audrey knew it her hand had made contact with his face. Jason's face went dead still; a look was in his eyes that brought fear to her bones. She drew back scared he might hit her back.

"I want you out of my house in the next thirty minutes." He went back inside without saying anything else.

Audrey silently went into the guest room and put Lulu back in her cage. She put on her jeans and tank top, and zipped her backpack up. Her stay turned out to be much shorter than what she'd expected. At least it was still light out. Then she could find a restaurant to sit at and think about what she was going to do next. Why had she slapped him? He was only telling her the truth right? She was a filthy prostitute who sold her body out on the streets. But why did his words provoke such anger inside of her? She guessed what she wasn't used to was that instead of coveting for her like most men did he cringed at her, and he was showing herself a mirror of what she'd become; a whore.

She came out of the room with her things, on the way out passing his room. His door was shut. She debated to knock to tell him sorry, but decided against it.

When she got to the living room Jason was standing there. She stood still. For a while neither of them said anything. Audrey yanked up her tank top to conceal more of her chest.

"Listen, before leaving I wanted to tell you I was sorry."

He said nothing.

"I'm not a violent person. Well, unless there's someone trying to attack me first." She trailed off. "But that's beside the point. I don't know what came over me to hit you like that. I really am sorry."

He still didn't say anything. She supposed he was only making sure that she was going to leave his house like he'd told her to do.

"Ok, well I'm leaving now. I truly appreciate you letting me stay at your home, even if it was only for one day it meant a lot to me."

Jason heard the sincerity in her tone. "Well, I guess since I am a Christian, I will forgive you this once."

"Thank you." She said.

"That means that you can stay." He told her.

Originally Jason really was going to kick her from out of his house. When she'd slapped him, though Jason would never hit a woman and didn't believe in resulting to violence, he at least wanted to shake some sense into her, it took everything in him not to. Nobody had ever put their hands on him before, not even his own parents had ever spanked him. He'd always thought of himself as a self-constraint type of person, being able to be a master over his temper, but when she hit him something inside of him went off like one hundred pounds of dynamite. It surprised even himself. But although she had angered him—which he wouldn't allow her to manipulate his emotions again, he wanted to defeat Mr. Thomson more and succeed in getting the executive pastor position. Mr. Thomson had shamed him in front of everyone, at least with Audrey it was just he and her as witnesses. That still didn't give her an excuse for her uncivilized behavior, but he was going to get out of her what he'd sought to. She was going to help him get that position.

Audrey wanted to jump up and down and hug him, but she kept her jubilant compulsion at bay and instead thanked him.

"Come sit with me at the dining room table once you've put back your stuff. I have some things I want to converse with you about. And remember to keep that thing of yours locked up." He pointed to Lulu.

After she put her things back in the guest room she sat with Jason at the dining room table. He placed a sheet of paper in front of her and a pen.

"This is a contract. I wrote one up so we can be clear on our prearrangement with one another and so we can form some rules."

"Ok." Audrey picked up the pen to sign her name on the dotted line.

"Wait, before you sign it we are going to go through it with one another."

He picked up his copy. "The first thing that I want to go over are the contents of the deal. The deal as I've mentioned to you before is that you get your life together and then testify in front of my church how I've helped you attain freedom and joy in your life. But you have to show you've been changed before going up in front of my church, so that part will have to wait for a while. They need to see evidence that you've really been transformed thanks to my help. One thing you will not mention when you give your testimony is that you stayed with me. You'll just say I was a great assistance to your process of transformation and that I won you over to Christ. Do you understand?"

"Yes, I do." Audrey nodded. So far this deal seemed like it was more for her advantage than his. She didn't know all about the Christ thing though. God probably wanted nothing to do with such a terrible sinner like her.

"Next are the rules." He said flipping his page over. "The first one is that you cannot continue prostituting any longer. Do you agree with rule number one?"

"I'd love to stop prostituting, you can't begin to comprehend how much I would, but how do you expect me to survive after my stay here is over?"

"That's the whole point of the deal. It's to get you cleaned up and to attain a new life, a new life which also includes you getting a new job. I will allow you to stay here until you find yourself a well-thought-of job and save up for your own place, all without pay. But there will be a seven month time cap to it all. Seven months should give you sufficient enough time to find a job and save up for a decent apartment. So you better look good and hard for one, and quick, because I won't be having you taking advantage of my generosity."

Audrey agreed. Allowing her to stay in his home for free until she moved out was generous. She still couldn't wrap her brain around the fact it was all for a testimony. He didn't want sex out of her, he wanted her to change her life around. But was Jason sincerely different from all the other men in her life she'd encountered who only wanted her for her body and pleasure? Why did he want her to change her life around? Could it be because he really did care for her poor, lost soul? Could someone want to help her for the first time in her life with no strings attached? Or was he was getting something out of it too?

"Why do you want me to change my life around so much?"

Jason was quiet before answering. "Because you need to." And he left it at that.

"Since you agree with rule number one, I will go on to rule number two. Rule number two is that you never put your hands on me again." He looked at her coldly. "It was ridiculous the scene you created. You need to control that flaring temper of yours."

Admittedly it was wrong of her to put her hands on him, Audrey could concur with that, but Jason was making it sound as if that scene was entirely her fault. He did speak down on her so harshly after all. Shouldn't he at least apologize for the part he had to play in it?

"Ok." She said with indifference. She didn't want to start another argument.

"And finally rule number three is that you never enter into my bedroom or try to come on to me again. Besides there's no way I'd ever want to lay with someone who used to be a nefarious, sleazy prostitute, even if I weren't a Christian man."

Audrey balled her hands into fist trying to keep her rumbling frustration inside. She was getting fed up with him speaking down on her and using his fancy words to do so. What did nefarious mean anyways? She knew whatever it meant it wasn't a compliment. "Well great, that makes the two of us. Because there's no way I'd want to lay down with you either, even if you paid me to do it." She couldn't help herself.

Jason shook his head. There she went again trying to provoke him to anger, but she wasn't going to get the satisfaction this time. "It's good to know we're on the same page. After you've signed the papers leave them at my door." He walked off and went into his room.

Audrey browsed through the job pages of the newspaper the following morning. She searched for whatever opening she could find, scrubbing toilets could be an option and she'd even take it. The sooner she could get out of this man's house the better. She didn't want Jason to think she needed him for anything or that she needed him to depend on. Audrey was well and able to take care of herself and that's what she was doing long before she'd ever meet him, she'd done it ever since she was fifteen years old. It also didn't appeal to her to stay in the house of someone who thought he could speak so negatively about her anytime he wanted to and for her not to dare say anything back about it. Some Christian man he was, all he did was hurl insult after insult at her. Audrey already knew that her life was wretched, there was no need for him to have to remind her of that depressing fact every single moment of the hour.

Going through the ads didn't help her much. Either they required you to apply online or in person. She had neither a computer nor a car and the clothes she had left were nowhere near professional.

Jason walked past the living room into the kitchen to pour himself a glass of water without saying anything. Audrey didn't notice though because she was diligently searching in the newspaper, looked like in the back near the job section. Good, so she'd taken his advice and got right to looking for a job.

"How's your search going?" Jason sat down on the other couch.

She looked up at him then back at the newspaper. "Good."

After that Audrey remained quiet like he wasn't there, maybe then he'd leave her alone. It was only a matter of time before he'd say something that would irk her nerves again. Right now she didn't want to be vexed by him.

"Where's that beast of yours? I hope you have it locked away."

"That beast name is Lulu and she's outside for some fresh air. I already taught her how to make her way back here. She's a really nice and smart cat if you'd give her a chance."

Jason didn't see why he needed to give her a chance. He already knew he hated cats and there was no changing that. He ignored her comment.

"So where are you from?" He asked her.

Her silent treatment wasn't working. It looked like Jason wasn't going to go away. Audrey gave out a heavy breathe. "Why the sudden interest?" Any other time he only had orders to give her.

"I think I should at least know some basic information about a person I'm allowing to stay in my house." He set his glass of water down on the coffee table waiting for her to answer.

"I'm from Savannah, Georgia."

"Is that currently where your family is?"

"I don't have a family." Audrey kept her gaze on the newspaper in the hopes he wouldn't pry any further than what he already was.

"What happened to them?"

The backstory concerning her life and family, Audrey never told anyone about, she even tried hiding her past from herself. Now he was getting too nosy for his own good.

Bitterness draped her speech when she said she didn't have a family. From her hesitancy to respond to his question Jason would do well to venture their relationship was not on good terms. "Did they disown you after you chose to become a low-down prostitute because they were ashamed of you? I mean if that's the case you couldn't blame them right? Naturally any parent would be upset that their daughter chose to live such an unethical lifestyle. I mean what could be worse than having a floozy as a daughter?"

Audrey closed the newspaper. This guy never tired of belittling her. She couldn't take any more of it and his over the top arrogance, thinking he knew everything about everything. It was about time for her to put him in his place.

"Before I became a prostitute my mom died when I was twelve and my dad left out of my life by the time that I was seven. I haven't heard from him since, I don't know whether he's dead or alive. So no I don't think becoming a prostitute had anything to do with it."

Audrey couldn't stop herself now. Her body felt fraught with a fire detonating inside of her and she needed to release it. "And while we're at it I told you already before I didn't choose to become a prostitute. I'm sorry that not everyone can have a perfect rosy life such as yourself since birth. You call yourself a Christian, yet you aren't very Christ like. Like Jesus taught aren't Christians supposed to treat others with love and kindness? All you do is condemn me. You act like you're so much better than others because you're privileged and so righteous. It's no wonder why you're not married yet, no woman would ever want you, and you probably don't have many friends, if any. I know that I've lived a disgusting and wretched life. I'm not proud of the things that I've done. You're so busy holding up a mirror to others well let me hold up a mirror to you. Your attitude is foul and you don't know how to treat people. You're mean, rude and unfriendly and I'd rather live on the side of the streets than to live another day here with you." By the time she was finished Audrey had tears of not only anger, but of hurt streaking down the sides of her face. Bringing back up the ill fate of her mother was too much for her to take. She'd spent so long trying to bury the memories.

There was deep anguish in her moist eyes that Jason could feel just by looking into them. His gaze fell to the table too taken aback to even reply. The velocity of his heart beat faster against his chest. Audrey really did hold up a mirror to him, and what she'd said had stung him right in his inner being. She had used the same exact word as Pastor James did when she'd called him unfriendly. Not only that, but her mother had died and her father abandoned her and he had accused them of disowning her. Maybe Jason really were all of those things people were saying about him. Maybe he was unfriendly, unapproachable and not relational.

Audrey quickly wiped away her tears with the back of her hand. Part of her felt good finally getting what she thought about him off of her chest. "I'll be getting my stuff and going now." She stood.

"No. You don't have to do that." Jason's foot started involuntarily bouncing. "I'm...I'm sorry." He said in a hushed tone.

Could Audrey's ears be deceiving her? Did she hear him say the words *I'm sorry*? And he actually sounded like he meant them too.

Audrey turned to face him. He could hardly get his eyes to look at her from the shame he felt. "I'm sorry. I spoke wrongly of you without knowing of your circumstances. I ask that you could please forgive me."

Audrey saw that he did seem like he was remorseful.

"Since I am a pretty merciful person, I guess I could forgive you this once."

Jason gave her a half smile, it was the first time she'd ever seen him give somewhat of a warm-hearted expression.

Chapter 8

It brushed against his leg. Its mouth wasn't making any movements, but somehow weird motor like noises erupted from its belly. Jason had been on the computer in his office working on some church projects when the thing snuck up on him and almost made him have a heart attack. Since four days ago when Audrey had showed him a mirror of himself Jason started being more friendly towards her the best ways he knew how, he'd helped her to find where to apply for jobs online and he'd even showed her how to make a resume that could result in her being more competitive than other applicants, but having her cat roaming freely around his house still didn't sit too well with him. He didn't believe there was a possibility he'd ever like cats.

Audrey knocked on his office door and peeped her head inside.

"Is Lulu in here messing with you? I can take her out if you want me to." She held her chuckles within. She'd been watching Jason for nearly five minutes as he kept shifting his legs from side to side as if he were playing a game of hopscotch in his attempts to prevent Lulu from touching up against him.

"I would greatly appreciate that, thank you. She's kind of distracting me from my work, and for some reason she keeps making these odd noises. Is she hungry or something?"

Audrey walked into his office and gathered Lulu into her arms. "No she's not hungry. She's purring, meaning she wants someone to show her affection." Lulu snuggled her head against her check and Audrey drummed her fingers underneath her chin.

Jason watched perplexed and slightly grossed out. He couldn't see how anyone could derive pleasure from owning a cat, they were clingy and bossy creatures.

"What makes you like cats out of all of the animals on the planet earth?"

"They're so furry and cute. How can you not like them?" She scratched behind Lulu's ears, her favorite spot. Her purring kicked into full gear, heightening to a whole other level. "Lulu in particular came at a time in my life where I was at the end of my rope. She was a stray kitten, still with her eyes closed and everything. I ran into her after a bad night on Lankford Avenue of being..." Audrey's eyes glazed. She didn't want to talk about that right. "Let's just say she came in my life when no one else was there for me."

The more Audrey revealed of her past the more Jason felt sorry for her. He didn't know what she was going to say, but how her eyes became saturated with distress made him not want to ask anything further about it.

"So you like to read a lot huh?" Audrey walked over to his tall book shelf changing the subject.

"Yes, I love to read. Ever since I learned how to read I've loved it."

"I bet your grades in school must've been really good."

"They were OK." For some reason her compliment caused him to want to respond with humbleness. In actuality Jason never made anything shy of a 4.0 grade point average on every one of his report cards. He'd also graduated valedictorian of his class.

"My mother used to read me bedtime stories all of the time when I was a child, at least in the beginning she used to." Audrey ran her finger up and down the spine of a book, but her attention was off somewhere else. Why was it lately she kept thinking about her past when all she wanted to do was obliterate it?

"Well anyways, I don't want to disturb you any longer while you're working. I almost forgot what I came in here to ask you about. Is it ok if I washed my clothes? All of the little bit of clothes I have are dirty."

"Sure, the laundry room is before you get to the garage. It will be the door to your right."

Audrey left his office with Lulu in hand and he went back to work. Jason was curious to know more about her past and how she'd found her way to Tampa but he could see how it affected her in a negative way whenever she'd bring it up.

Hours had gone by of him typing and creating ministry policies. His fingers were beginning to cramp and his eyes were becoming sore from looking at the computer screen for so long. He would have to finish for now and do the rest tomorrow. He was drained. Not hearing from Audrey for the last few hours he went to check on her to see if she'd found everything to be ok while washing her clothes.

When he entered into the laundry room there were suds seeping from the washing machine blanketing the entire floor. Audrey was in the middle of the laundry room using a mop to try and clean it up. Upon seeing him come into the room her eyes became bugged-eyed and she gave him a look that said *Uh-oh*.

"I'm so sorry. I read the instructions wrong and put in too much detergent." She bit her bottom lip.

Her bizarre expression alone would've caused him to laugh if he weren't so tired. "It's ok. When I first started to learn how to wash clothes the same thing happened to me once." He walked closer to help her get the mess up.

Audrey extended out her arm. "No don't step there, its liquid spilled over there."

It was too late. Before Jason could even take note of her warning his feet had already made contact with the slippery, gooey liquid. His feet slid and slithered as his hips wobbled and shook. He struggled to remain balance, but one thing led to another and his hands went flying in the air as he felt himself slipping backwards.

Audrey grabbed his hand to keep him from taking a plunge, but she came falling down with him too. When they hit the tile floor Audrey fell on top of him. He and her foreheads clashed together like cymbals.

Jason howled. It took him a few minutes to get over the initial pain gnawing at his back and forehead.

"I'm so sorry." Audrey put her hand on his forehead, stroking it with her thumb. The pain subsided some from her soft touch. She was still on top of him.

Jason slid his body from underneath hers and stood up. "It's fine." He rubbed his forehead.

Her touching him the way she did was too much physical contact for his comfort. He didn't want her to get any unreasonable ideas. He being more friendly to her didn't change the way he felt regarding his statement about not wanting to lay with someone who used to be a prostitute. And besides, he wasn't going to commit any sins against God. Whoever he was to lay with he would be married to her first, like his Christian faith required.

"Are you done yet?" Jason yelled aloud from down the hallway.

Jason glanced at his watch. He'd been waiting near about thirty-five minutes for Audrey to get out of the restroom so they could head on their way to the clothing store. *Geesh!* Did it really take this long for women to get ready? Hearing no response Jason tapped his foot. He'd give her another five minutes.

He poured himself a glass of water and drank it, washing it out after he'd finished. During that time frame four minutes had passed. He'd had enough of waiting. Jason walked up to the bathroom door, lifting his hand to knock on it. Audrey opened it before his hand touched the door.

"I'm done now. Goodness gracious be patient. A girl's supposed to have as much time as she needs to get ready." Audrey joked.

Jason looked at her face. Layers upon layers of makeup was coated on it. "Is all that really necessary?" He pointed at her face.

"What? Is it a sin for me to wear makeup too?"

"I didn't say that. But if you're going to wear it why use so much? And why use such dark colors? You kind of look like one of those crazy gothic chicks." He sported a playful smile.

Oh so dorky man had a sense of humor and wanted to try and roast somebody with it today? Audrey could say a lot about his attire and how he always wore the same dorky style every day, but she wasn't going to make fun since she was in such high spirits. She smiled at him, letting him have this round.

When they got to his car an elder lady walking her pet poodle waved over at Jason from the side of the road. "Hey Jason, how are you doing?" She talked with a slow raspy voice.

From her warm smile she seemed like she could be one of those old ladies that portrayed the grandmother role to everyone, even to those she didn't know. There was something familiar and neighborly about her to Audrey.

"I'm good Mrs. Hanson, how are you doing?" Jason called back while unlocking his car door, hurrying to get in. He could already tell from Mrs. Hanson's upright posture and the squinting of her eyes that she was burning to ask who Audrey was.

Instead of continuing her walk like Jason had hoped she would Mrs. Hanson took it upon herself to meet them in his driveway.

"And who is this beautiful young lady?" Mrs. Hanson smiled over at Audrey.

Great, how was he supposed to answer to her? Jason opened his mouth to say something, but nothing came out.

"That's so kind of you. My name is Audrey. I'm Jason's long lost sister." Audrey saved Jason the trouble.

"Wow." Mrs. Hanson's eyes enlarged. "I didn't know you had a sister Jason."

"Yeah, well we've recently reconnected. I'm always getting on his nerves. Right Jason?"

Audrey nudged him in his side with her sharp elbow. Jason kept his grunt inside. "Yes, indeed you are."

Mrs. Hanson laughed at them as if they were her grandchildren. "Well that's great to reconnect with loved ones. My name is Mrs. Hanson, but feel free to call me Grandma Hanson." She pinched at the air as if she were pinching Audrey's check. "I live two houses down from here. You can come visit me anytime you'd like and I'd be sure to cook you up something mighty good. I tell Jason to come for dinner all of the time, but he never does."

"I'm sorry Mrs. Hanson. I've been pretty busy lately." Jason said.

"Well just know the door is always open for the both of you."

Mrs. Hanson smiled at them.

When they arrived to the clothing store Audrey strolled up and down the hallways at least five times through each one of them, Jason following behind her. He couldn't understand for the life of him why she kept going down the same hallways as if something she didn't see before was going to magically appear on the racks. Her face was in deep thought like she was having a hard time making a decision.

"What's the issue here? If you don't see anything you like then we should leave. We've been in this place for over an hour now." Jason hurried her.

"That's not the issue. I see plenty I like, it's just that I want to be sure to pick out clothes that are cute yet at the same time appropriate. You know what I mean?" Audrey thought that he out of all people should understand where she was coming from, since it was he after all who got on her so bad about her attire the other day.

Her goal was to find outfits that could be both professional and modest, not wanting to choose anything that was too exposing. Looking for clothes of that fashion was completely out of her zone considering she used to be a prostitute. The clothes Audrey was used to shopping for were anything that had less material and revealed the most. Now she was searching for clothes that were the polar opposite so she was finding it to be a bit difficult.

"How does this look?" She held up a black dress with ruffles along the neckline. It was cute, professional and not to mention modest like Jason seemed to like. Audrey was pretty proud of her pick.

Before Jason could say how he felt about it someone called out his name in the store. Audrey looked along with Jason in the direction of the person who had said his name. It was a young woman. She was tall and slender with black hair and honey brown skin, and she dressed really prissy like she was the Queen of England. Even how she walked with her chin high in the air let it be known that she thought she was of royalty.

"Hey Jason. Long time no see how are you doing?" She gave a shy smile.

Audrey could tell that she was going to greet him with a hug, but Jason looking stiff and awkward shook her hand instead.

Jason couldn't believe it was her. As soon as he'd saw her his heart started fluttering faster. Rebecca Rice was someone he used to have a fancy for. She attended his church for over four years before moving to New York to go to college. She was the only other woman besides Cindy he thought was worth liking. She was a Christian woman, modest and refined. She was also ambitious. Before she'd left for college they'd worked together in ministry for a while and from there on he'd began to grow feelings for her, though he never told her this.

"Hey Rebecca." Jason cleared his throat. "I'm good. How are you? I thought you were still in New York City for college."

"I actually have recently finished up my bachelor's degree so I'm moving back here to Tampa. It's crazy living up north. I was happy to come back home down South." She put her hand to her mouth giggling.

"That's great. I know your parents are happy that you're back as well." Jason wanted to tell her he was happy to see her back too, but his nerves got the best of him so he stood still and didn't say anything else.

Audrey watched the embarrassing scene unfold before her very eyes. It was apparent Jason had a thing for this girl, but due to his lack of social skills with women he didn't know how to properly convey his feelings. After a very long and awkward silence Rebecca glanced at Audrey as if she'd just noticed she was there.

"Oh, how rude of me, I didn't see you standing there. My name is Rebecca." She looked Audrey up and down before giving her a limp handshake with her pinky finger extended. "Nice meeting you."

"My name is Audrey. Nice meeting you too." Audrey presented a small nod of her head. She didn't quite know what to make out of Rebecca's prissy personality, but maybe she could be a nice girl if she got to know her a little better.

"Is she a friend of yours Jason? I've never seen her at church before." Rebecca fished for answers.

Audrey thought to tell her she was his long lost sister, but seeing how they knew one another from church Rebecca would more than likely know it was a lie.

"Yes, she's a friend that I'm helping out." Jason had no choice but to tell her the truth. Rebecca already knew all of his family.

"Oh, that's nice." Rebecca smiled with her lips pressed tight together.

She kept giving Audrey subtle scrutinizing looks that Audrey didn't receive as favorable. She wondered if Rebecca had a thing for Jason too and was being watchful because she thought something more than a friendship was going on between the two of them.

"Yeah we're friends, but he's more like a brother to me. And I'm like an annoying sister to him." Audrey added hoping it would give Rebecca some clarity that there was no romancing involved in their relationship.

Audrey saw Rebecca's eyebrows rise a little higher, not looking at all convinced by her words. Rebecca's expression communicated to her that she was after Jason and Audrey had better not get in her way. That was fine by Audrey because Jason was someone who'd be placed at the last on her list of men to date, he actually wouldn't even be on her list at all, so Rebecca needed to direct her combative attitude somewhere else. Audrey wasn't looking for a fight. Rebecca could have him.

"Well Jason we must meet again. I'm just now settling back in, but I will start regularly attending Waters of Life one of these Sunday's. I'm so excited to see you and everyone else again. Here's my phone number so we can catch up." Rebecca gave Jason her phone number and hugged him, Jason still appearing uncomfortable as he hugged her back. There was at least eight inches in between them as he gave her a one arm hug with a light pat on the back. Before leaving, Rebecca was sure to fling knives at Audrey with her threatening gazes. Rebecca looked like she meant war.

Audrey shook her head amazed. Hopefully she hadn't just found herself being thrown against her own will into a game of tug-of-war.

Chapter 9

For the rest of the entire week Jason was in such a joyous mood that Audrey had even stopped hearing him complaining about Lulu wandering about everywhere in the house. Throughout the evenings Jason would walk around the house smiling, continually checking his cell phone, no doubt to see if the duchess had called or texted him. He was inattentive to anything else. In fact when she thought on it more Audrey had become almost nonexistent to him as well. During the majority of the day he would spend his time in his office, coming out only for something to eat or to go to his church for meetings or whatever other work he had to do there.

Audrey continued to apply and search for jobs, but no one had reached out to her yet for an interview. Her confidence in being able to secure a suitable job began to dwindle, not comprehending what she was doing wrong. Maybe it was due to her lack of experience. She had none she could put on her resumes. The only job she ever knew was prostituting and she was sure that wouldn't be beneficial if she put that on her applications.

She wanted to find a job in a hurry so she could save up to find her own place. It would only be a matter of time before Jason and Rebecca became a couple and then he'd give her the boot, which was understandable. Audrey didn't want to be a thorn in Jason's side preventing him from pursuing his love interest.

Feeling her stomach performing it's Olympic worthy somersaults again she went into the kitchen to search for something to eat. In the cabinets were foods to make spaghetti. Spaghetti seemed easy enough to make.

"I knew I smelt something about to burn." Jason came in the kitchen and stood behind her. "You have the sauce cooking on too high. You're supposed to let it simmer on low to medium heat for a while."

Audrey turned the stove knob down lower, feeling a bit worthless she couldn't even make spaghetti right.

"Well it still tastes pretty good. Here, try some." She scooped some in a spoon and held it to Jason's mouth.

Jason kept his mouth firmly shut shaking his head no.

"Come on, please." Audrey made her bottom lip droop. "I didn't put my mouth on it if that's what you're worried about. Please just try it."

Rolling his eyes Jason gave in to her imploring and opened his mouth. Audrey excitedly inserted the spoon and watched for his expression.

Jason rolled the sauce over on his tongue refraining himself from spewing it out.

"So how is it?"

"It's bad." He said forcing himself to swallow down the rest.

"Are you serious? But I did everything the instructions told me to do. I made for certain that I did it step by step this time."

"Yes, I'm serious. That sauce is devoid from any hint of flavor. Luckily I came just in the nick of time to save it from being scorched, but even then it's not any good."

"What am I doing wrong?" She slouched her shoulders.

"Here, move aside." Feeling somewhat sorry for her pitifulness Jason took the spoon from her hand and stirred the sauce. "Let me help you out and show you how it's done."

When it came to cooking Jason seemed to be a natural pro at it. As he cooked and demonstrated to her how to make spaghetti Jason schooled Audrey with some cooking 101 lessons. He filled her head with knowledge concerning the different spices and herbs to apply to a dish based on its specific cuisine. He taught her about marinating meat, stuffing meat, baking meat, searing meat and everything else concerning meat. Audrey knew she wasn't going to be able to remember it all, but she endeavored to retain as much of the information he was giving to her as she could.

The delectable smell hovered around the kitchen as Jason neared finishing the spaghetti. The savoring aroma caused Audrey's mouth to salivate.

"Since I cooked you can go and set the table while the breadsticks are finishing up." Jason told her after he'd prepared two exquisite plates full of spaghetti with the sauce layered flawlessly on the top.

Audrey quickly grabbed the plates; she was over and above eager to eat. If the food tasted anything how it looked then she knew it was going to be divine. When she was finished setting the plates and silverware on the table she sat down in front of her serving. She licked her lips eyeing the plate in front of her. Everything looked so good she couldn't wait to indulge herself. Five minutes had gone by. Jason was taking too long making those breadsticks. Many times Audrey had to stop herself from grabbing her fork and diving in before he came. Another few minutes passed. Audrey stood about to discover what was taking Jason so long.

Without warming Jason appeared behind her and set the tray of breadsticks on the table.

"I'm sorry was I taking too long for you?" He raised his eyebrows. "A man's supposed to have as much time as he needs to finish what he's doing. Or does that only apply to females?" Jason smirked.

"Ok you got me." Audrey sat back down trying to stop herself from grinning. "I'll work at being faster next time when it comes to getting ready."

"Good." Jason nodded.

Audrey picked up her fork and dug it deep within her spaghetti. She could see the stem still rising from the sauce. This was the moment she'd been waiting for.

"Wait." Jason said as the fork was inches from Audrey's mouth. "We need to pray first."

"Oh, of course, I guess I got a little carried away." Audrey placed her fork down.

They bowed their heads and closed their eyes. From hearing him pray Audrey could tell that he did it a great deal from how it came so fluidly out of his mouth. Audrey couldn't remember the last time she'd prayed, which was not something she was proud about.

After Jason was through praying Audrey picked up where she'd left off and took her first bite of the spaghetti.

Jason watched her as she took her first mouthful, observing if she'd like it. This was his first time he'd ever cooked for anyone so he was curious to know a second opinion concerning his cooking. Her eyes rolled to the back of her head as she started doing some sort of dance in her chair, swaying her body from side to side.

"This is soooo good! It's like a party of flavors doing a dance inside of my mouth. You're a great cook!" Audrey quickly helped herself to another mouthful.

Jason chuckled as she did yet another dance. "Thank you."

The following moments that passed not much was to be heard from Audrey, aside from her fork clinking loudly against her plate as she consumed mouthful after mouthful of her spaghetti.

"I'm stuffed." Audrey leaned back in her chair, placing her hand on her belly.

She'd eaten everything on her plate including two breadsticks in a time span of no less than five minutes. It was a sight for Jason to witness seeing someone with such a small frame as Audrey being able to devour so much food in so little time.

"You ate as if the food was going to run away from you." Jason peered down at her empty plate. Not even a string of a spaghetti noodle was left on it.

"I guess I was really hungry." She shrugged.

"Anyways, how does a woman not know how to cook?" Jason messed around with her.

For a while Audrey didn't say anything.

"My mom died before I learned how to cook from her, though she never really did cook much, especially after my dad left us. Ever since her death I've been getting by mostly on ramen noodles and microwavable foods." She paused. "Actually this is the first real home cooked meal I've had in a very long time, so I thank you for you being kind enough to cook it."

Jason's eyes fell down to his plate, sympathy tugging at his heart for her misgivings. "You're welcome." Jason said in a quiet tone.

"So how did you learn how to cook? Did your mom or sisters teach you?" Audrey asked aspiring to lighten up the mood. Her intentions in telling him that wasn't to throw herself a pity party or to gain solace from him.

"No, I don't have any sisters, just one older brother. How I learned to cook was a bit by reading cookbooks, but I learned the majority through practicing and through trial and error."

"I should start reading those books too. Maybe I could learn a thing or two for myself." Audrey said. "By the way I've noticed that you have a huge TV in your living room going to waste. It's never turned on. Don't you ever watch any television?"

"No, I prefer to keep my eyes shielded from the nonstop trash that appears on it."

"Even still you can watch DVD's of your choice and monitor what you want shown on your TV or not. Sometimes watching a movie can be relaxing and fun."

"I guess…but who wants to be bothered going through all of that. Its better just being turned off."

Jason's phone vibrated against the table. He reached for it so quick that in the process his fork fell to the floor. After he'd picked it up he checked his cell phone hoping it was her. Four days had gone by since she'd last contacted him. Since running into her that day she'd send him text messages, usually asking how his day was going and telling him about her stay in New York. Yesterday he'd texted her good morning, but she never replied back. He opened his messages. It was Patrick, the youth pastor, asking him about a budget proposal for an event.

All in twenty seconds time alone Audrey saw Jason's expression go from optimistic to a look of dejection. Maybe the duchess had told him something he didn't like. Jason placed his phone back down and said nothing else as he finished the rest of his meal.

"So I've noticed you've been in a particular good mood lately ever since we ran into that Rebecca friend of yours at the clothing store." Audrey said attempting to cut the mounting silence that had formed.

"You seem to be noticing a lot of things lately…but yes; it does make me happy to run into an old friend."

"Do you like her?" She saw the look of surprise on Jason's face from her question. Audrey knew it was blunt but it was no need beating around the bush.

"Well, she is someone to be admired." Jason couldn't help but to smile as he confessed.

Although Rebecca didn't treat her friendly to say the least, Audrey was glad to see Jason so happy. He seemed to really like her a lot.

"Have you told her you like her yet?"

"No." Jason sighed.

That figured, Audrey thought. Jason didn't even know how to hug a woman without making it look like he was hugging a hideous, giant toad. Audrey guessed it was her turn to help Jason out by offering him a few tips when it came to the woman department. "Because you cooked for me tonight and you've been helping me out so much I will help you learn how to win the affections of a woman ok."

"Are you joking with me right now?" What kind of advice could she possibly give him? Jason didn't think Audrey's scandalous approaches on attracting the opposite sex were ways he would find very useful. He'd prefer to keep things holy how God wanted him to.

"No I'm not joking. Really I can help you, and there's no sin involved. Just some helpful tips and that's all." Seeing she'd caught Jason's attention Audrey continued. "Ok so the first thing to learn is how to greet a woman." She stood up. "Show me how you greet a woman that you're interested in."

"What on you?"

"Yeah on me, who else is here?" She looked at him waiting for him to get up. Jason stood not hiding his displeasure of her making him participate. "Alright now show me."

"Give me your hand." He told her.

Audrey reached out her hand and then he shook it with a loose grip. Even as he shook her hand he looked sick.

"That's how you greet a woman you like?"

"Well exactly how else am I supposed to greet her?"

"Giving her a hug would be nice. And I'm not talking about a hug that's over the top." She said after reading the look of "*Are you crazy*" written on Jason's face. "But a hug that's sweet and to the point that says you're special to me. When you hug her place your arms around her torso and lay your hands on the middle of her back, this position conveys to a woman that you want to support her and be that comforter for her. Your bodies don't have to be pressed so tightly together, but be close enough as to where you don't make her feel like you think she will give you the cooties."

"Here." She stepped closer to him reaching out her arms. "Try it on me."

Jason backed away from her the second she took a step closer to him. Giving her the same harsh recoil he'd given her in his car that night.

"It's ok, I get the point." He frowned.

His face said it all to Audrey. In his eyes she was still a nasty ex-prostitute that he didn't want to touch in fear of impurity. His recoil still had the same effects on her as it did the last time.

Embarrassed she looked away from him and then down at the table. "Ok that's good that you understand. From now on greet Rebecca that way ok and she'll fall for you in no time."

Audrey grabbed her empty plate not understanding why she felt so dirty all of a sudden. "I'll wash the dishes." After picking up Jason's plate she left and went into the kitchen.

When Jason was finished doing his ministry work he needed to do on his computer he came into the kitchen and poured himself a glass of water. Soon he would need a secretary for all of the paperwork the church gave him to do. Running three big ministries all by himself was beginning to take its toll on him. Not eating anything all day he pulled out a tray of thawed chicken from his refrigerator to prepare to bake it. He counted making sure it would be enough for him and Audrey in case she wanted some too. Jason hadn't cooked for her again since that night a week ago due to his busy schedule. He didn't mind cooking for her, and seeing Audrey's silly expressions when eating his food were entertaining, but he also didn't want Audrey getting used to the idea he would become her personal chef.

Though strangely Jason had noticed Audrey was acting different around him. Instead of lingering around him to chit chat like she'd normally do she would leave the main living room whenever he appeared. Could she not be feeling well?

Jason knocked on her bedroom door waiting for her to give him the ok for him to come inside, but he heard no answer. Pressing his ear to the door he couldn't hear anything on the other end so he twisted the door handle.

When he pushed opened the door he saw Audrey sitting up at the foot of the bed. She had quickly placed the covers over her legs upon him entering through the door.

"I told you to come in, but I guess you didn't hear me." Audrey didn't look up at him. She kept her eyes on the floor, and from the way she spoke with her head hanging low she sounded depressed.

"No I didn't hear you. I'm about to cook a meal and was checking to see if you wanted some too?"

"No thank you."

Jason noticed that her eyes were puffy and wet. "Are you ok?"

"I'm fine thanks."

"You don't look fine to me." He walked in front of her.

As he did Audrey clinched the covers around her legs. Her face showed that she was in pain though she was trying to hide it. Jason pulled the covers away from her and found what Audrey was attempting to conceal. Her left foot was swollen and bruised.

"How did this happen?" Jason's eyes widened as he bent down on his knees to inspect her foot.

Audrey didn't say anything. She even pulled her foot away from him and placed the covers over her legs again to hide it. It looked like there was something she didn't want to tell Jason about. Something that she maybe wasn't supposed to do. At the possibility of it being her sneaking out at night to go to Lankford Avenue Jason felt himself getting angry. Why was she trying to go back to that filthy way of living again?

"What is it that you're not wanting to tell me Audrey? And how did you get that bruise on your foot?"

Jason remained silent giving her time to answer, but she still didn't say anything making him become even more frustrated. "I told you already I will have no hooker living under my roof!"

"It's not that." Audrey's voice cracked. "Lulu hasn't come back since Monday, so the last few nights I went out looking for her. Last night I slipped on a hill and hurt my foot."

"Why didn't you tell me?"

"I didn't want to bother you, you've been so busy. And besides it's not like you care about Lulu anyways."

Jason put his head down feeling in error for talking too fast and accusing her of going to Lankford Avenue. And even though he may not like cats he didn't wish anything bad to happen to Lulu. Jason knew the strong attachment Audrey had for that cat and how much it meant to her.

"Still you should've told me so I could've helped you look for her. Maybe it would've at least prevented you from getting hurt." He took the covers from off of her legs again. "Here give me your foot so I can see what's wrong with it."

"I wouldn't want you to get infected." She scooted her foot away.

"What are you talking about? This isn't contagious."

"I know that I'm a plague to you and that you don't want to touch me. And its ok I get that."

Confused Jason thought about why she was acting the way she was. Had he told her he didn't want to touch her? Jason thought about the night when he'd backed away from her when she'd told him to hug her. Now that he thought about it, her strange behavior had started soon after then. He looked into her eyes which showed she was wounded not only on the outside, but also on the inside too. He didn't know his reaction had caused her internal distress.

Audrey scurried closer to the edge of the bed. "I need to go and find her. She needs someone to look after her, someone to take care of her." Her bottom lip trembled. "I don't want Lulu to be alone."

"Are you crazy? You can't go out searching for her like this. Do you see the poor state of your foot right now?" Upon seeing her eyes water Jason said comfortingly. "She'll come back don't worry."

After he'd wrapped an elastic bandage around her ankle Jason went back into the kitchen to put the chicken back in the refrigerator for another time. Audrey had insisted she didn't want anything to eat. By that time night had fallen. Jason grabbed a flashlight and went out to look for Lulu. He snuck out quietly not wanting Audrey to find out. He didn't want her to get the misconception that he might've actually liked the fury creature, because that couldn't be anything but further from reality. Jason's sole reason for wanting to find Lulu was because Audrey's sulking around was beginning to set a gloomy aura around his home. He didn't want it to feel like he was attending a funeral service everyday due to Audrey's depressive state.

He searched up and down the road shining the flashlight in bushes or dark ditches that Lulu could've gotten stuck inside. He did this for forty minutes up until his legs grew weary of walking, having circled the neighborhood three times already. Flickering his light down a steep hill he caught a glimpse of movement. Keeping the light directed towards its attention he found that it was Lulu. Feeling more excited than what he thought he'd feel to find her he carefully made his way down the hill at the same time calling out her name. With success he made it down the hill, but Lulu made no efforts to come his way despite him calling her name. It looked like he was going to have to pick her up, causing him to make contact with it, which was something Jason never wanted to do with the creature. Sighing Jason walked over to her stretching out his arms. Lulu ran away from him as if he were a stranger and like she hadn't spent over a month in his house by now. Jason was sure he was going after the right cat.

In his pursuit of chasing her Jason's foot landed in a muddy puddle. He fell smack on his rear-end creating such intense pain he had to refrain himself from roaring out loud in the still night. He had half the mind to just let the thing run free and for it to never return again, but then he forced himself up thinking about Audrey. After five minutes of chasing the God forsaken thing Jason had finally caught it.

"You listen here Lulu, don't you ever run off like that again, you hear? Audrey was so worried about you." Jason said holding Lulu in his arms while walking back to his house. Surprisingly its fur felt like a soft pillow against his skin.

Audrey awoke from her sleep in the middle of the night, her foot throbbing, though it wasn't the pain of her foot that had caused her to wake up. She heard noises coming from the front door. Rich neighborhoods weren't exempt from getting robbed, if anything that's where the robbers felt like all the money was. Feeling alarmed she hobbled out of bed onto her good foot. She knew Jason had told her to stay from out of his room at all times, but concerning the urgency of the matter she opened his door to notify him that a burglar was trying to break into his home.

Switching the lights on in his room revealed a spotless and sizable space. The interior was decorated with all black. Audrey's eyes went to the king size bed. Underneath the silk white covers nobody was there. Her legs trembled. Where had Jason gone? Could it be him coming through the front door? She peeped her head in the living room concentrating her eyes to distinguish who had just come from through the doorway. The figure humped over and released something from out of its hands. It didn't take Audrey long to discern it was Lulu from her skittering strut, giving it away that it was her.

With joy consuming her she ran over to Lulu and cupped her into her arms. "Lulu where have you been? Why did you make me worry like that, huh?" As Audrey stroked her behind her ears Lulu hummed and vibrated like an electric generator.

Jason remained still hoping Audrey would forget he was there and go back inside of her room with Lulu. She was so entangled with pampering Lulu he thought that was what she was going to do, but then she put Lulu down and looked his way.

"Jason, that's you over there right?"

He didn't want to say anything, but seeing that he'd already been found out Jason turned on the living room lights.

Audrey beamed at him with overwhelming elation, thankful Lulu was safe and Jason had found her. Before thinking about it she went closer towards him with her arms outstretched to give Jason a hug to show him her gratitude. Then she stopped a few inches shy of him remembering the last time she'd tried the same thing and the disapproving reaction he'd given her. She wanted to respect him by keeping her distance so instead she thanked him.

Jason saw her hesitancy to hug him. Her head hung low from humiliation as she told him thank you. Surprising himself he closed the distance between them, pulled her body into his and wrapped his arms around her.

She stiffened in his arms, shocked by not only his gesture, but how extremely warm it felt to be in his arms. Her heart began to speed up as Jason rubbed his hands between the middle of her back causing the hairs on her neck to rise.

"You're not a plague Audrey." Jason whispered in her ear.

How he said her name so soft and affectionate caused a heat wave to surge throughout her whole body. Jason pushed his body away from hers and looked at her with longing eyes. Audrey's mouth became dry.

"So how did I do?" Jason cracked a smile.

"Wh…What?" Audrey said confused by the sudden mood change.

"Did I do the hug right, how you told me to do it?"

It dawning on her that it was all just an act Audrey got a hold of herself. "You're supposed to do that on Rebecca." She felt her face getting hot and looked away in order to hide it from Jason.

"Well, you're the one who told me to do it on you the other night. I was just getting in some practice." Jason said with a light laugh. "But concerning Lulu, it was nothing. I just didn't want it to feel like I was attending a funeral everyday by seeing you moping around. I'm going to bed now." Jason yawned.

Audrey stood in the spot he'd left her, her heart still walloping away in her chest. She went to bed that night feeling confused with her influx of emotions regarding Jason.

Chapter 10

Men were all scum. That was Audrey's final say so on the matter. It was no use in believing they could prove her otherwise. When Jason had hugged her that night she almost opened herself up to him because he'd done a kind act by finding Lulu for her. But even then, he'd said it himself that he'd only did it for his benefit because he didn't want to see her moping around. For a brief moment being held in Jason's warm arms she'd thought some feelings were developing for him, but she couldn't allow her silly emotions to get caught up again like they did when she'd met Cash. Men were all the same and all that came out of trusting them was disappointment.

Jason reached out his hand for Audrey's. "Let us bow our heads in prayer first."

She placed her hand in his and bowed her head as he led in prayer. It didn't help alleviate her emotions any that Jason was being super nice to her lately, and that he would cook for her too whenever he made a meal for himself. Men had been nice to her before, but he was being nice without asking anything in return from her. Tonight he'd made steak, mash potatoes and roasted vegetables.

Audrey took her first bite of the steak and her eyes almost watered from how delicious it was. "Wow this is by far the best steak I've ever had." This was actually Audrey's first time having steak, but she knew it had to be the best from how good it was treating her taste buds.

Jason smiled from her rave review.

"How's your ankle?" He asked her.

"It's feeling much better. The pain has almost completely gone away now. I think I should be able to walk on both of my feet again soon." Or at least Audrey hoped so. She was tired of hopping around on one foot and being confined to stay sitting down all day.

"That's good. Just remember to keep your foot elevated or reclined, in that way it will help to drain fluid from the injury. And don't put any pressure on it either because that'll only cause it to get worse."

Audrey nodded her head impulsively. She'd heard him say the same thing over and over again about twenty times already.

Before he forgot Jason dug into his pocket and handed Audrey the cat collar he'd brought for Lulu earlier that day. "While out shopping today for the cat food you told me to get, my eyes kind of landed on this, so I thought it'd be good to get one for Lulu. I went ahead and got it customized in that way if she were to ever get lost someone would know who she belongs to, and I wouldn't have to go through the chore again of finding her. Until you get your own phone number I put mine for the time being."

Audrey took the collar in her hand. It had a silver heart charm with Lulu's name inscribed on the front, and on the back was Audrey's name and Jason's cell phone number. The collar was a pretty sky blue. Sky blue used to be Audrey's favorite color.

She didn't know why Jason was being so kind or why she felt an emotion she couldn't pinpoint budding inside of her, but what she did know was that men were all the same. She had to keep whatever she was feeling in line so it wouldn't lead her to the same demise as it did in her past. Men were all the same and there was no denying that.

"What?" Jason said to her, interrupting her thoughts. Had Audrey said that last part out loud?

"Did you just say men are all the same? What do you mean by that?"

"I meant to say thank you." She said hoping that it would end the conversation. Audrey looked at Jason, who was still waiting for her to explain what she meant about the men were all the same part. From what she read from his firm demeanor he wasn't going to give up until she answered his question. "My mind was thinking about all of the men I've come across in my past is all." She let out a small sigh, knowing her statement would only lead to more questions from him.

"And what about all the men you've come across in your past?"

"Just that their all flesh craving beast, who only want women for their pleasure and to use them for all that they can get out them." It was no use in her hiding from Jason how she sincerely felt about his kind, and rightfully so. She was only presenting him with the facts.

"Well, I can assure you I'm not like all the other men you've met before. Some of us men are decent. It may be rare to find, but there are still some of us good one's out there."

"Oh, really? Men all want the same thing. I've never met a single one who couldn't be seduced."

"Well, I can't. To some guys life is not only about seeking pleasure from women."

Audrey stopped cutting midway into her steak, the thought just now really occurring to her. "Are you by chance, still a virgin?"

Jason slowly wiped around his mouth with a napkin before answering. "Yes, and it's not something I'm embarrassed to admit."

So that explained why he had no knowledge when it came to interacting with women. Nevertheless Audrey was still stunned to find out he'd kept himself a virgin all the way up until the matured age of twenty-seven-years-old.

"Though, at first I used to be." Jason felt his leg began to twitch underneath the table. Whenever this subject came up he'd always get uncomfortable, but for some reason right now he felt like he should articulate to Audrey his Christian morals and what he believed in. "I was home schooled up until the age that I was fourteen, so when I started to attend a public school you could imagine my eyes were opened to a lot of things. I didn't know that many guys practically worshipped it. Their reaction when I told them I was still a virgin was anything far from a pat on the back. In fact I became an outcast at school, not being able to really fit into any sect or group of people. I was the *"weird guy"*. For a moment I really started to question my faith because all I had ever known since I could remember was church every day, and sacrificing. God was what I was raised to believe in ever since I could learn to understand the English language. I think the first word my dad ever taught me to say was probably Jesus." Jason chuckled and then his expression became serious again.

"I began to think my life was unfair. How was it that everyone else could do whatever they wanted to do without a care? How could they continue on sinning and not feel bad about it? But then I started praying to God more and my relationship with Him grew deeper than ever before. He allowed me to understand that the sacrifices were worth it, that it's a beautiful thing being able to call myself His child and that He loved me more than I could ever imagine."

Audrey saw great passion in his eyes as he spoke about God. It was an indwelling passion that she'd never seen before in a man's eyes. She felt her tear glands flutter and then closed her eyes wondering where that'd come from.

"He also let me realize that s…sex is supposed to be sacred, a privilege, in which He designed for married couples. And that it's not just some audition for dating or something to be had with anyone carelessly. As a Christian man who loves the Lord with my whole heart, waiting to make love in a pure, intimate, and undefiled way until I'm married is not optional for me. For me, who has chosen to live my life as a Christian it's a decree, and it's a gift from God that I take very seriously. And His ways are much better than the world's. The world's way only brings about lewdness and no real commitment. So I've come to understand and appreciate my worth more due to waiting, by knowing that no one can have the most intimate part of me, by becoming one with my flesh, besides the one I choose as worthy enough to be called my wife first."

Audrey blinked her eyes again suppressing the tears that were residing on the surface. She'd never heard a man speak like that before regarding sex. "That's great you had such great discipline to wait for so long." If only Audrey would've had the choice.

Jason nodded his head. It was pretty righteous of him. "I'm not going to sit here and lie to you though. There were times when I wondered how it might feel, but I've learned to push those thoughts aside until the appropriate time comes until after I'm married."

"Well, I wouldn't know how it feels either." Audrey forked around her vegetables trying to tame the emotions she felt stirring inside.

"What? Haven't you laid with many diff—?" Jason stopped himself seeing the upset look on Audrey's face.

"No its ok, you're right." Audrey nodded with a sad smile. "Of course as a prostitute I've slept with so numerous of men, I'm afraid I can't even count, but even then I can't say I've ever experienced the beauty of what you've just spoken of. I learned to shut my mind off when it happened. I never got into prostituting for the pleasure of it.

There was never any pleasure in it for me."

Audrey wanted to grab at her chest from the excruciating agony brewing in her heart, but she kept it inside. Every one of her most horrible memories that she'd tried to bury deep away within her were becoming manifested before her eyes.

Even though she was looking down at her plate Jason could see a tear streak fall from down her face.

"Audrey, are you ok?" He leaned toward her concerned.

"I'm fine." She said trying to calm herself down.

"You don't look fine to me."

"Really, I'm ok." She placed her fork down. "After eating I've become sleepy. I'm going to head to bed early tonight." Audrey excused herself from the table and walked briskly on both of her feet, forgetting her sprained ankle was still not fully healed yet. She almost fell, but thankfully the wall was right beside her, hindering her fall.

Jason stood in a hurry upon seeing her sway and reached out for her. "Audrey, are you sure you're ok? Do you want to talk about whatever that's eating away inside of you?"

"No! Please, just let me go to sleep now." She stood on her good foot and limped away.

Audrey couldn't go to sleep that night. The nightmares kept her awake the entire time making her break into sweats. Why had she revealed so much to Jason? And why had she allowed those memories to reemerge? If there was one thing she could be certain about was that she wasn't going to allow it to ever happen again.

Jason picked up the change in Audrey's disposition much quicker this time around. She had become distant towards him. She didn't say anything at all to him throughout the day, and she even had declined him every time he'd offered to make her a meal. He knew it had partially to do with her past that she didn't want to talk about. Realizing it was such a heavy weight on her made him begin to look at her in a different light. He didn't just feel pity for her anymore, but now he also wanted to help her break free from her hurts for some reason. During his prayer time he'd even received the impression from God to begin praying for her more. Maybe that had something to do with it. His father taught him once that when a person begins praying for someone so much, God begins to place in the person's heart the concerns that He feels for the individual.

Today she was in the living room for the first time in days, browsing through the newspapers in a wearisome state of mind. He could tell she was becoming frustrated that her job search kept coming up empty handed.

"Hey." Jason stood in front of her. She looked up from her newspaper like she'd just noticed he was there.

"Hey." She muttered and then made an attempt to get up, trying to avoid him again.

"Wait." Jason stopped her. "Let me see how your ankle's doing."

Before Audrey could open her mouth to tell him no, Jason sat down on the coffee table and took her left foot into his lap. He then rubbed his fingers at the bony parts of each side of her ankle, making smooth, flowing movements causing whatever pain she might've had to magically disappear. The only thing she felt as he massaged her ankle was warmth, which sparked from her leg and issued out through the rest of her body. Wherever Jason's fingers touched, her skin throbbed. He applied light and pleasant pressure around her ankle then moved his hands up and down the outer part of her calf. Her body reacted to his touch in ways she'd never experienced before.

Audrey pulled her leg away feeling ashamed and disconcerted. "That's enough." She took a breath inside hoping she could conceal the bodily enjoyment she'd felt away from Jason.

"Does it feel better now?" Jason asked her. From the nonchalant look on his face she could tell that he was clueless.

Relieved he hadn't noticed Audrey tried to bring herself back down to normal again. "Yes it does. Thank you." She wiggled her left foot, it really did feel better. Jason seemed to be good at everything. "How do you know so much about how to take care of a sprained ankle?"

"I wanted to become a doctor once." Jason smiled. "I was actually going to school to become one, but God had it planned another way. I even got accepted into a medical school of my choosing, but I ended up stopping at my Bachelor's degree to go into ministry full time."

"Were you regretful about it?" Audrey asked after some silence had passed.

"I don't know." Jason shrugged. "I mean I've wondered from time to time what it would've been like if I'd chosen the doctor route instead, but I've come to like where I am now. And whatever I do, whether it's being a doctor or a minister, I figured it's just good to prove my abilities, to show others that I can perform with greatness in any position given to me."

Jason thought about the Thomson's and others who'd like nothing other than to see him fail. When the time came they would witness his greatness and how he could outperform them at any level. Soon Audrey was going to have to show that she was being transformed so they could follow through with their deal. Days were going by quicker than he'd noticed.

Audrey gathered up her newspaper. "Well, I'm going to go fill out some more applications on the computer."

"Wait. Why don't we watch a movie first? I thought of a good one that we can watch together." Jason had already planned this movie since yesterday, hoping that by her watching it she could better understand his faith and open up to him more about her past.

From the way she gawked at him wide eyed he knew she was caught off guard by his suggestion.

"Well wasn't it you who said that watching a movie can be relaxing. It looks like you could use a breather."

Audrey gave in and Jason put in the DVD. As the movie started Audrey slid farther to the edge of the sofa. She wasn't expecting Jason to sit on the same couch as her. It was starting to get more difficult to be around him while trying to keep a cap on the emotions for Jason she couldn't quite understand herself.

From the opening scenes of the film she could tell that it was going to be one of those Jesus movies. Although it wasn't something she was too excited about, something drew her into the movie that made her keep her eyes glued to the screen.

In the movie Jesus preached that he was the way, the truth, and the life, in the face of being cursed and slandered by the mobs and Pharisee's. Even though she'd read the Bible, watching it come to life on screen had a profound effect on her. Jesus spoke invigorating words that roused her spirit to yearn on the inside. He said there was a better way of life by choosing him and that he could make old things new and forgive everyone from all of their sins committed, no matter how vast and great they were, so long as the person believed in Him and repented. He performed miracles by causing the blind to see, the sick to be healed, the weak to be strong and the broken to be whole. Towards the end of the movie he was beaten so badly that on parts Audrey had to shield her eyes and when they nailed his bloody and battered body on the cross she wept.

Jason heard Audrey's sobs as she broke down beside him. He, himself was trying to keep his own tears in. Although he'd seen the movie many times by now, he'd always get teary-eyed during this part of the movie.

When the movie was over Audrey wiped at her wet eyes, staring down into her lap. She didn't say anything for a long time.

"Is...is it really true?" Audrey finally said.

When she looked into Jason's eyes there was pain and

desperation in hers so intense, that not being able to withstand it he let his gaze fall away from hers.

"Is it really true that God can make a person new?" Audrey's voice broke." That he can free a person from their past that's filled with hurt and shame, no matter how many unthinkable sins they committed?"

"Yes." Jason bobbed his head earnestly, fully believing that God could free anyone so long as the person desired Him to. He wanted Audrey to believe so as well, and that she could be free.

"I want to be free."

"And you can be free Audrey."

"I want to be free from Jade." A tear fell from her eye.

"Who's Jade?" Jason asked her confused. This was the first time she'd ever brought up such a name.

"Jade. Jade is a devil. She's a devil who has chained me and won't let me free."

For the next hour Jason listened to Audrey as she divulged to him her life's story. A story that was so heart wrenching he wouldn't have thought a person could've been able to live through.

Chapter 11
Audrey's Past

Everything wasn't always all bad in Audrey's life. There were times when she would laugh and have fun like the normal kids her age did. Though those moments were far and in between she still had glimpses of them in her memory that she still held dear to her. Like when her mom, Sabrina, who Audrey was told she looked a splitting image of, would take her to the corner store every Friday after school was over to buy her a bag full of penny candy. Or the time when it was her fifth birthday and her mom baked a strawberry cake for her, done her favorite way, with real strawberries glazed on the top. And when her mom and dad would watch cartoons together with her, Audrey snuggled in her dad's firm arms and her mom stroking her hair, as they laughed. Her dad worked a lot, but every day after work he'd come home with her a toy or some candy. And one Christmas he'd taught her how to ride a bike without the training wheels on, always being patient whenever she fell off the bike and encouraging her that she could do it if she'd just keep trying, and she did with his help. They'd go to church together nearly every Sunday and her mom would read her the Bible at nights. Those were the moments of the good times she remembered the most.

Their little family of three had made a nice home for themselves. It wasn't anything fancy or spectacular, but it was nice, and it was what Audrey called home nonetheless. They lived in Savannah, Georgia, where Audrey was born and raised. As far as she could recall the only family she knew was her mother and father. And at first Audrey thought this was normal until kids at her school told her stories about their aunts, uncles and grandparents. When she asked her mom about it Sabrina responded by saying she was the only child so that's why Audrey didn't have any uncles or aunts, and concerning her grandparents Audrey had none, and it'd be best if she didn't ask her anymore questions concerning them ever again. Audrey later found out that her grandparents had disapproved of her mom being with her father, Wayne Mitchell.

When Audrey's parents got together her mother had only just turned sixteen and her dad was twenty-five. Her mom was raised by devout Christians so they disapproved of their relationship right from the get go, believing her father was much too old for their young daughter. Sabrina rebelled against their commands to stay away from him and ended up pregnant by him out of wedlock at the age of sixteen. Her parents threatened to have Wayne sent to jail so before giving birth to Audrey, her dad and her mother ran away together and settled in Savannah, he promising to marry Sabrina when she turned the legal age. And he did marry her when Audrey turned three.

In the beginning her parents used to be happy all of the time, but then the arguments started. At first just here and there, but then they escalated into an every night affair. She heard them at nights through her thin bedroom walls screaming at one another. She heard her mom say one time while yelling at Audrey's dad that her parents were right about her should've staying away from him, and that he didn't know how to keep his pants on. After the endless nights of yelling matches and break ups to make ups her dad stopped coming home at night's altogether, leading up to their divorce when Audrey was seven-years-old.

It happened one day out of the blue when her mom packed their things saying they were leaving their home, her mom's explanation being that her father was a no good dog and that he'd found himself another hot young thing to occupy his time with. Audrey cried wanting to at least see her father one more time before they'd left, having not seen him in over a month already.

"Come on Audrey." Her mom yanked her in the car as Audrey kicked and shouted. "You're no good of a trifling dad doesn't want us anymore. He's left us, so there's no reason for us to keep staying here."

Audrey couldn't believe what her mom had told her. How could her dad not want her anymore? Her mom must've said something mean to upset him again. Audrey knew they'd be back together again and that her parents would make up, just like the previous times. Her mom had to be lying, dad would never leave them. Audrey's hopeful thinking turned out to be in vain though, because her mom left that day and they never returned to their home again in Savannah. After that they moved to another city, Audrey couldn't even remember the name of the city because they didn't stay there for long. They went from place to place, moving around frequently. Her mom claimed it was because of her not being able to keep a job. Due to this reason Audrey was never able to make real friends or get fully accustomed to one town.

It wasn't until Audrey was nine that she thought her mom seemed like she was going to finally stick to a place. Audrey had even made a friend next door named Asia. Audrey hadn't had a friend in a long time, since they lived in Savannah. She and Asia would go to the playground together in the neighborhood and climb on the monkey bars, and Asia would share her food with Audrey whenever she didn't have anything to eat because her mom couldn't afford to buy grocery majority of the times.

Two years had passed since Audrey had last seen her dad, and she missed him so much, hoping he'd come and find them and they'd be a family again. But as time progressed Audrey realized what her mom had said about her dad was true; he'd left them and forgotten about them.

Her mom began to act differently towards her too, becoming bitter and cold like she hated Audrey's existence. She'd turned to alcohol to ease her pains and even once let it slip out of her mouth when she'd gotten drunk one night. Her mom let a lot of things slip when she got drunk.

"Why did I have to disobey my parents and get knocked up by that fool?" Her mom cried while laid out on the couch of their small two bedroom apartment, the liquor bottle still clutched in her hand. "I know it must be God punishing me for my wrongdoings. Now I'm miserable, stuck here with a child I don't need or can take care of, and my dad won't take me back."

"Mom, I can take care of you." Audrey covered her mom's body with a blanket. She didn't understand why her mom was saying such mean words concerning her, but she wanted to make her mom happy again like they once were before.

"How you going to take care of me, huh?" Her mom mumbled before she closed her eyes and drifted off to sleep.

In the end her mom settled in Houston, Texas. When they moved there she never talked about Audrey's father again. It was like he was dead to her.

Her mom started seeing other men and would leave Audrey home alone when she'd go out on dates with them. She began to see her mom less and less. Her mom never read her the Bible like she used to, neither did they go to church anymore. And when Audrey would try to get her mom to read her a bedtime story as an excuse to just spend some time with her, her mom would always tell Audrey no or to leave her alone.

"Audrey I don't have time to read you anymore of those fairy tales. It's about time for you to grow up anyways and realize that the world is not anything like those books you want me to keep reading you." Her mom looked at her with solemnness. "The world is cruel Audrey. And you'd better get used to it so you can survive."

Her mom went from different men regularly like the day changed to night. She never stayed with them for long and she didn't bring them to the apartment much either—that was until Audrey's mom met Mike. The moment he first came through the door that day, Audrey knew she didn't like him. He was a buff, strong man with a bald head. The aura surrounding him was unpleasant. Audrey was playing with her baby doll, a gift her dad had given her, when they came through the front door. When Mike saw her sitting on the floor Audrey saw fire flicker in his dark brown eye's like a devil.

He bent down in front of her. "My, my, my so this must be the little Ms. Audrey, I hear yo mama talk so much about." He smirked at her. "You look just like her too, pretty and all."

Audrey played with her doll trying to ignore the man, him being so close to her made her skin itch. His odor reeked and his breath smelt of alcohol.

"Girl, how old are you?" His voice was loud and commanding.

"N-nine." Audrey murmured.

"Aren't you a little too old to be still playing with them baby dolls?"

"That's what I keep telling her too." Her mom said with a slurred speech. Audrey knew she had to be drunk. "It's about time for her to grow up. I keep telling her that. But Mike, leave her be and come follow me into the bedroom." Her mom smiled while ushering him over with her index finger.

Before getting up to follow her mom in the room, Mike smiled down at Audrey with his black lips and winked at her.

The following months Mike and her mom did that same routine often. Audrey would go outside in the yard so she wouldn't hear them when they made noises. She'd sit outside all day on a tree stump and look up to the sky, thinking how her life used to be when she and her mom were still with her dad. Either no kids lived in her small neighborhood or their parent's never allowed them to come outside because Audrey had never saw any kids to play with.

She lifted her hand to the crystal blue sky. When she looked into the heavens she felt free and at peace. Going outside to look at the sky became a ritual for Audrey, a way for her to escape from her loneliness. When looking at the sky, she felt like she was somewhere else, somewhere better.

"God, are you there?" She held her hand to heaven. Her dad had told her once that heaven was where God lived and that because she believed in Jesus and was a good girl God would hear her whenever she'd pray to Him. "Could you please bring my dad back?" She'd say in tears while gazing into the sky every day.

Unfortunately for Audrey, after a year went by her mom and Mike got married. Not long after they were wed did she begin to notice drastic changes in her mom. Sabrina who was usually so beautiful and full figured began to waste away. Dark circles formed underneath her eyes and her nose was always runny. Her skin began to sink into her hollow face. She'd appear so horrible that at times Audrey would be afraid to even look at her.

One day sitting on the living room floor while watching TV she heard her mom and Mike arguing back and forth in the bedroom.

"I need more Mike." Her mom sobbed.

"Sabrina, you are already taking too much too fast."

"I don't care! I have the money so have Clement to bring me some more."

Mike gave out a disgusted sigh. "I told you before you buying it from Clement that heroin is an extremely addictive drug and that because of that reason I don't even take it, but you didn't care. Now you're like this, shaking all of the time with spit foaming out of your mouth. You should've just stayed with smoking weed."

At the time Audrey wasn't exactly sure what heroin was, but she promised herself she'd stay away from it so she wouldn't end up like her mom.

From then on her mom got worse, and she'd stay out much longer during the day. Audrey would stay outside until she came home because she didn't like being in the house alone with Mike. He'd be there after he'd get off work, sitting on the couch smoking. The way his piercing eyes studied her whenever she looked his way made her feel uncomfortable.

One late afternoon it was nearing dark and her mom still hadn't come home yet. Audrey sat on her tree stump as the sun began to set. The blue sky was now turning gray.

She heard the door open behind her and her body went numb,

knowing that Mike was standing behind her. She stayed facing the sky hoping he'd go back inside after checking up on her.

"Come on inside Audrey, its dark out now." His rugged voice resounded.

"I'm waiting on my mom."

"I don't care who you're waiting on. It's dark outside and I said to get inside now."

The tone of his voice was so threatening it caused Audrey to get up in fear of what he might do to her if she didn't obey. When she got inside of the house she immediately went into her bedroom and shut her door. She lay on the bed waiting to hear her mom come home, but after waiting for thirty minutes she'd found herself dozing off to sleep.

The sound of her bedroom door knob twisting open was what woke her. She thought it was her mom, but then as her eyes became focused in the dimly lit room she saw that it was Mike. He was standing over her bed gazing down on her with those devilish eyes of his.

"I've been having my eyes on your pretty little face for a while now Audrey." He licked his lips.

Audrey was frozen with terror. She didn't like the way he was looking at her like he wanted to eat her up.

"Yo mama told me you were becoming a woman now and that you'd started your period last month." He pulled something from out of his pocket. "Do you know what this is?" He grinned at her. Audrey didn't say anything and he ripped it open. "It's called a condom, and I'm going to teach you how to put it on me so I can help you to grow up. It goes down here." He pointed below his stomach and Audrey turned her head away.

She swallowed then managed to open her mouth to speak. "But I…I don't want to. I don't want to grow up. I don't want to put it on you."

"It's no need for you to be afraid, pretty girl." Mike said as he unbuttoned his shirt. "It won't hurt. I'll make sure that it doesn't. It'll feel good to you I promise."

But Mike had lied. It didn't feel good at all to Audrey. The pain was excruciating. And he never stopped when she cried and begged for him to. She was only eleven-years-old then, and as early as eleven was she already being taught on how to please a man.

After he'd finished satisfying himself with her that night, Mike told her to get cleaned up before her mom came back home. He also warned her she'd better stop her crying, and before he'd left her room to wash her bedroom sheets he threatened Audrey that if she told anyone about it he'd kill her.

Depression took hold of Audrey daily following that night. She'd cry in her room and stay up all night fearing Mike would come through her door again. For the next year he didn't. Because he'd found a job as a truck driver he began to be home rarely, giving Audrey somewhat of a relief. Audrey never told her mom about the night Mike had raped her, not only because she was afraid, but because part of her didn't think her mom would care or believe her. Her mom hardly even acknowledged Audrey's existence anymore as it was.

Her mom became another person, who no longer smiled at her or hugged her. Audrey missed her old mom; the mom who used to show her love and affection, the mom who used to gently untangle her long hair after she'd shampoo it for her, and the mom who used to tell her that Audrey was her sweet princess, but those precious days were long gone.

It was storming and raining real hard one night. The wind howled against Audrey's window preventing her from staying asleep. From the crack of her bedroom door she saw that the living room light was still on. Her mom complained about the bills enough so Audrey went into the living room to turn them off.

When she went into the living room her mom was humped over sleeping with her face down on the coffee table. Audrey neared closer to her to wake her and then discovered that there was a needle protruding from her mom's arm. She shook her mom's shoulder over and over but she wouldn't wake up. Feeling panicked Audrey swept her hand over her mom's face to remove the hair that covered it. From just one look at her mom's distant eyes that were sunken in let Audrey know that she was dead. Her mom was blackening skin and bones. She would never get the atrocious image from out of her head and what sadness her mom's eyes held even after death. The coroner said it was a drug overdose and she'd been dead for not too long, although she'd looked like she'd been dead for days already.

Audrey blamed herself thinking maybe if she'd went into the living room a few moments earlier she could've saved her mom from overdosing. For days Audrey couldn't sleep or eat. She felt like she wanted to die too. The two people she'd loved the most in the world had left her.

When her mom died Mike had come home from driving trucks for a while and had her mom cremated. She never knew what he did with the ashes because he never told her. Audrey wanted to run away, but she knew no one and had no place to go. She was only twelve and didn't have any money or a job. The thought of having to stay with Mike from then on petrified her. But maybe he'd leave her alone like he'd done for the past year. Hopefully he wouldn't touch her again.

"I'll take care of you from now on ok Audrey." Mike told her three days after her mom had passed away.

He was sitting on the couch her mom had died on with his head leaned back. Audrey hadn't seen him in months before then. She'd noticed he'd grown a rough beard and it had gray hairs in it. His eyes were blood red and he looked tired. This was the first time he'd said anything to her since he'd been back, and Audrey preferred to keep it that way, but today he'd called her into the living room saying he needed to talk to her about something. Audrey sat on the small couch to the right of him and remained quiet. Maybe if she didn't say anything he would hurry and finish with whatever he wanted to tell her so she could go back inside of her room.

"You know, I loved yo mama so much." He looked over at her with droopy eyes. "But she never loved me back. She still loved yo daddy." He said with spitefulness. "She only wanted to use me as a way to escape from her pain and I let her because I loved her, but no, she didn't love me." He shook his head. "She just loved the drugs that I could get for her."

Mike downed the rest of the can of beer in his hand and crushed it before throwing it on the floor.

"You know…I love you too Audrey." He smiled at her and Audrey's stomach turned. "You're so pretty, just like yo mama used to be when I first met her. I couldn't resist myself that night. I did it only because I love you." Mike sat up in his chair. "Why don't you come lay down with me tonight and make your stepfather feel better."

The next three years the sexual abuse and rapes continued regularly when Mike would come home from off of the road. He'd always use the excuse that he loved her, making Audrey sick. It wasn't until she was fifteen-years-old that Audrey decided she couldn't take any more of it. She dropped out of school and got the bravery to run away while Mike was away working on the road one day, not caring how she'd survive, as long as she didn't have to endure Mike sexually abusing her again.

She lived on the streets for three days eating what she could out of trash cans and using public restrooms to freshen herself up. It was some of the worst days of Audrey's life, but she refused to go back to live with Mike. Anything was better than returning to live with him, and being the girlfriend that he pretended Audrey to be in his messed up head of his. Well at least she thought anything was better, that was until she met Cash.

Audrey was digging in the trashcan of an alleyway for scraps of food one day when she felt him tap her on her shoulder. When she turned around to face him the first thing she noticed about him was the angel wing tattoos on his neck and his friendly smile. He was a young man, probably twenty-five at the time, with silky hazelnut skin and dark brown eyes. He kind of had a virtuous appeal going on for him.

"What is a pretty girl like you digging in the trash can for?" He smiled down at her.

Audrey didn't say anything, being caught off guard.

"My name's Cash, what's your name?"

"Au…Audrey."

"Well Audrey, do you need any help? I can help you get out of this way of living."

"I don't want to have to do anything bad." Audrey took a step back, thinking the man might've wanted her to steal things for him.

"Oh no, it's not like that at all." Cash chuckled. "It's just that whenever I see someone in need I do my best to help that person. I guess you can call it being a good citizen. We can be like best friends. So what do you say?"

"Just friends?" Audrey asked him. The thought of having a friend appealing to her, she hadn't had a real friend in a long time. She simply wanted a person she could confide to and lean on.

"Of course…just friends." Cash nodded.

The next few weeks Cash took care of her like a father would his little daughter, by buying her food and clothing. He seemed interested to know about her and help her out in any way he could. He'd even let her stay in his apartment where she'd sleep on the couch and he'd sleep in his room. He never touched her. She thought he was an angel sent from God to help her, but one day things changed and Cash took off his mask, showing Audrey the real him.

"Look Audrey, you see this bill?" He held the papers up to her face. "It's a light bill for nearly four hundred dollars. You've been burning up all the electricity."

"I'm sorry. I can turn them off earlier from now on."

"No, that's not going to help Audrey." He shook his head with a livid expression on his face. "There's also the clothes I bought for you and the food; that money all adds up. I can no longer afford it by myself. You need to get a job. I think you're beginning to take all the nice things I do for you for granted."

"That's not true." She shook her head. "I can get a job and help out. I'll look for one tomorrow at the mall." Audrey said trying to find a way to make Cash not mad at her anymore.

"No. Looking for a job like that will take too long. I need money now. Besides, I have a better job already lined up for you." Cash's eyes scanned her up and down. "I think you'll do well at it too, since you're a really pretty girl and all." He paused. "Audrey, you ever had sex with a man before?"

Audrey clinched the edge of the sofa, not liking where the conversation was going. "I...I was raped by my stepfather." She almost cried when she remembered the times Mike had repeatedly forced himself on her. She thought Cash would show her some sort of remorse by dropping the subject, but what he said next she would've never expected.

"Good, you have some experience then." Cash gripped her from the back of her head and pressed his lips hard against hers.

Audrey turned her head away frightened. "I thought you said we could just be friends."

"You ever heard of being friends with benefits?" Cash's lips curved upward like the Joker's and he kissed her again.

Audrey struggled to get free from him, pushing her hands into his chest with all her might, but he was too strong for her. She dug her nails deep in the skin of his arm and he withdrew from her yelling in pain. Before she could get up to run Cash backhand slapped her in the face with so much force she fell over on her side and onto the couch. Cash got on top of her pinning her down with his weight and squeezed his hand tightly around her neck. Audrey was so scared she thought she was going to die. She couldn't even muster words to come out of her mouth to beg him to stop because he choking her so hard blocked her airway, preventing her from speaking.

Cash leaned in closer to her with a smug smile on his face. She'd never seen such evil in a person's eyes before. If Mike was a devil then Cash was Satan.

"Audrey, I'm never letting you go, so it'd be better for you not to fight against it. You understand?" Cash tightened his hand around her throat firmer. "I said do you understand?"

Audrey strained to nod her head. Cash then removed his hand from around her throat.

"That's a good girl." He ran his finger around her neck. "From now on you listen to everything I tell you to do and you'll be fine...."

Cash buttoned up his shirt after he was done with her. "You were like a dead fish. I'll teach you how to better please a man in due time." He looked over her way. "Audrey what's your favorite color?"

"Blue...like the sky." She sniffled while trying to keep herself from crying. She was afraid Cash might hit her again if she did.

"Wrong answer." He moved his face close mere inches to hers, staring into her eyes with a frown on his face. "You're favorite color is Jade. And that's what we're going to call you from here on out. You understand? You're Jade now, and I'm going to make you one of the best prostitute's in Houston."

After that Cash did as he said he would, Jade was birthed and he became her pimp. Cash laid her down the rules about prostituting done his way. She was to work on the streets and make friends with no one. Audrey was to never kiss a man or to do any other thing that included using her mouth, and she was always to use a condom. He said if he was going to keep getting pleasure from out of her for himself as well he didn't want to catch any STD's, and that if he did get one from her he'd kill her.

Three days later Audrey was sent out to work on the streets for her first time ever and after that night was over with she wished she would've never been born. The experience was awful. Men would take her into their cars and do whatever they wanted to her, and she couldn't do a thing about it to stop them. She came home crying begging Cash if she could stop being a prostitute. After he slapped her around a few times she knew never to ask him about it again.

The longer Audrey stayed with Cash the more he knew how to get into her head and manipulate her. He'd become her worse fear, coercing her to do anything he wanted her to do. If she didn't do the things he demanded of her right at the second he wanted her to do it he'd beat her, sometimes until she'd almost lose all consciousness.

When she was working on the streets men told her she was pretty all of the time, but Audrey never felt pretty. She felt ugly, from the outside in. Cash had destroyed whatever self-esteem she might've had left, telling her she wasn't worth anybody's love, and that she wouldn't amount to anything. He would tell her she was only good at one thing and that was prostituting, and that she was only good at it because he'd trained her well. He told her nobody could take care of her like he did and that if she'd ever leave him he'd find her.

She was like Cash's property. He'd use her for anything, getting out of her what he could. One night she came home after a long day of being on the streets, trying to meet her quota so Cash wouldn't beat her again. She was tired and sore. Cash forced her to wear stilettos every night, which were eight inches high saying it'd attract more customers, so her feet were constantly aching her. All she wanted to do was to go to sleep and forget about everything. When she entered through the door Cash was already standing there waiting for her.

"You made what you were supposed to make tonight?"

"Yes." The way it escaped Audrey's lips like it was something to be proud of repulsed her. She'd really settled into the life of being Jade despite not wanting to.

"Well, hand it over."

Audrey gave him the bag of money and he lifted it in his hand as if he were weighing it. She walked past him to go to sleep before the pain in her lower stomach area brought her to her knees. Cash grabbed her by her arm.

"Did I tell you that you could walk off yet Jade?"

"No, I'm sorry." She put her head down hoping he didn't want to do anything to her that night. She didn't think she could take it.

"My buddy is in the room in the back. I told him for his birthday tonight you'd do whatever he'd like for you to do to him, except for those things which are listed in our guidelines of restrictions of course."

"But Cash, I'm hurting so bad right now." Her eyes watered.

He grabbed her chin in his hand and squeezed it so tight causing her to wince. "You think I care if you're hurting or not? You're going to go back there and do your job, unless you want me to give you the beating of your lifetime."

When she went into the back room she discovered that Cash's buddy had also tagged along three of his own buddies. They handled her so aggressively that Audrey couldn't go to sleep that night due to her being in so much physical pain.

As time went by the beatings Cash gave her got worse and his treatment of her grew harsher. When Audrey turned sixteen she looked for a job behind Cash's back so she could save up secretly and move away on her own, somewhere far away where Cash couldn't find her. She didn't have any decent clothing so coming into the interviews with little to near nothing on didn't go over well for her. No place hired her. She began to settle again, taking the abuse and pain, believing that her fate would consist of her being Jade for the rest of her life.

One day when Audrey didn't make her quota, Cash beat her so bad when she returned home. He squeezed the both of his hands around her neck choking her until she lost consciousness. It wasn't until after she'd woken up from off of the floor, bloodied and bruised, that she thought if she stayed with Cash any longer he was going to kill her soon. He wasn't in the apartment at the time so Audrey searched his room and found the stash of money she'd sold her soul to the devil making for him.

She took it and ran. At first she didn't know where, but for some reason something in her mind told her to go to Tampa, FL. Though maybe she'd chosen Tampa for its sentimental value; her parents said they were born and raised there up until they ran away. She took buses and hitchhiked until she found her way there.

Because Tampa was a brand-new place for Audrey, she went there thinking she could pursue a better life, a life in which she could rid herself of Jade and start with a clean plate, but that didn't happen. She found herself right back on the streets again because it was the only way she knew how to make money.

Being on the streets of Lankford Avenue was no better than when she was back in Texas, actually it was worse because she had no pimp to protect her from other pimps, but Audrey was determined to make it on her own. She didn't let anyone know she didn't have a pimp and she learned how to build her own client base without the help of one.

Audrey ran into Mama B in her second week on the streets and from there on she took Audrey under her wing until Audrey learned the ropes of Lankford Avenue, kind of being a safeguard for her along the way. But Mama B. couldn't shield her from everything. Audrey had the worst nights on Lankford Avenue. One day she almost got busted by a cop, but he made a deal with her he wouldn't lock her up in exchange for free sex. And there was this one time when a guy drove up to her and drug her in his car with four of his other friends. They brutally had their way with her and beat her, making her do things she'd never done before and things so sickening she didn't even want to speak of. That was the night she'd reached her last straw and decided to end her life to free herself from the misery, until she saw Lulu on the side of the streets.

Cash had turned out to be right about her after all. Being the prostitute Jade was the only thing she was good at. And Audrey had become real good at becoming Jade too, playing the part for men and shutting her mind off during the process so she could feel nothing but numbness from the guilt, degradation and shame. She was dead and empty inside. She wasn't a good girl anymore like her dad had once told her she was. God wouldn't want to talk with her anymore. She'd become the whore Cash designed for her to be, named Jade, and Jade was never going to let her go.

Chapter 12

Audrey could hear Jason turning the pages of his book while sitting on the other couch as she rubbed her fingers in Lulu's hair. Although he was turning through the pages Audrey knew he wasn't reading the words that were on them. She could feel his eye's on her. Ever since she'd told him her story he'd give her these sad looks all day like he pitied her. She wanted him to act like his normal self again and stop making her feel like she was a patient with some incurable disease.

"Why do you keep looking at me like that?" She caught him before he could look away at his book again. "I'm not dying or anything. And it makes me feel worse."

"I'm sorry." Jason's eyes fell to his book. "I can't help it."

When Audrey had told him about her past, he felt himself crying on the inside and almost had showed it outwardly, but Jason wasn't much of a crier so he held it in. He couldn't believe all of the abuse and tribulations Audrey had went through. No wonder why God had laid it on his heart to pray for Audrey more. Now, more than ever Jason wanted to help her to become free from her past like she wanted to. He didn't want her to suffer anymore.

"Why don't we watch a movie? It could be a funny one." Jason said wanting to do something to uplift Audrey's down in the dumps mood. "This time you can choose whichever one you'd like." His face became stern. "As long as it's not rated-R and has no vulgar scenes in it though."

Audrey smiled. There was the Jason she'd become to know; the one who was firm, yet learning to become a little more gentle while still standing faithfully on his principles. "Sure." She nodded.

After he'd found the movie on Netflix Audrey had suggested they should watch, he joined her on the couch she was sitting on. The emotions she couldn't understand still flickered inside of her sometimes whenever he'd get near to her like they were right now, but Audrey was becoming better with how to control them. She had to remind herself Jason was just helping her for the time being—five more months to be exact, and after that he probably wouldn't have anything else to do with her again.

As the movie unfolded Audrey would laugh hysterically at the comedic parts. Slapping her thigh and hunching over as she laughed. She was making so much movement that Lulu moved from off of her lap and onto his. Jason allowed the fury creature to stay lying on his lap since he could understand where Lulu was coming from. Audrey was kind of overdoing it with the laughs, but at the same time he was happy to see her smiling again.

"Oh, I'm sorry." Audrey said to Jason.

At first he thought she was apologizing for laughing so loud causing him not to be able to hear what the actors were saying, but then her gaze fell down to Lulu lying in his lap.

"I can move her from off of you if you want me to."

"Oh, no it's ok. She's asleep and I wouldn't want for you to have to disturb her."

Audrey stared at him with wide eyes and then gave a small smile before petting Lulu lightly on her stomach. She went back to watching the movie again and Jason relaxed as he watched it with her. To Jason the movie wasn't all of that funny, but he found Audrey's snorts to be humorous.

Audrey habitually reached her hand down to pet Lulu again like she'd been doing throughout the movie, but didn't feel Lulu's fury body in Jason's lap anymore. Instead she felt something else. Her eyes went to her hand. It had landed on Jason's lower part. She looked up at Jason whose eyes were as big as the moon.

Audrey snatched her hand away. "I'm so sorry Jason. I didn't mean to do that at all. I thought Lulu was still sleeping on your lap." She bit her bottom lip. "I'm so sorry."

Jason felt all the blood rush in his body like crashing waves, it had to be because of the shock right? He rubbed the back of his neck with his hand. "It…its ok. I know you didn't mean to."

"Are you ok?" Audrey examined his face, he looked like he was about to collapse onto the sofa.

"Yeah…I just thought about something I need to finish for the teen's ministry. I'll be in my office for a while." He got up.

Jason stayed in his office for the rest of that night, never coming back out to finish the movie. At first Audrey thought things were going to be awkward between them after that, but gladly the next day Jason came around to being his regular self again.

When Jason had went into his office after the little incident that occurred with Audrey, he had a hard time calming his boiling body down and he didn't know why. He felt his pulse vibrate everywhere inside of him, especially at the place she'd accidentally touched him at. The way his body was behaving was unfamiliar to him. There was no way he could've felt any morsel of pleasure from that…from her. He thought he must've been going crazy.

Determined not to confuse his shock with feelings of affection towards her he concluded the best way to handle the situation was to remain the same towards Audrey. It'd be best that way so Audrey wouldn't get any ideas which didn't synchronize with his. Even though he wanted to help her, because of the Lord had been placing it in his inner being to do so, Audrey wasn't the type of woman he'd ever find himself interested in. She might've been forced into prostitution, but that still didn't change Jason from not wanting to be with a woman who'd already slept around with so many different men. Everyone had their preferences and that was just his. The type of women Jason liked were the ones who'd kept themselves pure like Cindy and Rebecca.

He was in the living room reading a novel when Audrey ran from out of his office jumping up and down excitedly.

"Guess what! I just received an email saying that I got an interview for a job opportunity on Thursday!" She clapped her hands together.

"Are you serious?" Jason jolted up without thinking. He was so elated for her, knowing how long and hard she'd labored for this chance.

He walked towards her and wrapped his arms around her giving her a homely, congratulatory hug. Though a bit surprised at first Audrey placed her arms around his shoulders and hugged him back.

Jason held her for three seconds longer and took note of how he felt when hugging her. His body remained normal. He felt the same as the last time he'd hugged her when he was only playing around with her. He felt nothing. Good, so it was just the shock of what had happened that was getting to him the other day. He wasn't going crazy.

The position she was going to be interviewed for was to become a customer service specialist for a retail pharmacy. The day before the interview she and Jason did mock interviews with one another. He went over common questions with her typically asked during interviews and equipped Audrey to give the best responses. They picked out the attire she would wear to look professional and printed out her resume.

Jason drove her to the pharmacy on her interview day. During the whole drive Audrey played with her fingers. Her stomach was bubbling inside from her nerves. She gazed out the window to find something to distract her from the anxiety. Audrey looked at the trees, the road, and the sky, anything to try to tame her frizzled mind, but it was no use.

"Don't worry Audrey. We practiced for hours. You're going to do great." Jason encouraged her.

"Thank you." She took a deep breath and mentally went over the advice Jason had given her during the mock interviews.

They pulled into the driveway of the company. Jason switched off the ignition and turned to face Audrey. She couldn't see it, but he was nervous on the inside for her as well. He wanted her to succeed so she would get the job, so she would know she could be good at something else besides being Jade and that she was worth more than what she thought of herself.

"Well…I guess I'll be going inside now." Audrey reached to open her door.

"Wait." Jason grabbed the both of her hands in his. "Let's pray first."

Jason closed his eyes. "Father, I pray that you be with Audrey in the interview and that you place favor upon her to receive this job.

When she might not know what to say during the interview bring it to her memory what to say and speak through her so that she may find favor in the eyes of the hiring manager. I pray that you calm Audrey's nerves." *And mine too*, he thought. "In Jesus name. Amen."

Audrey got out of the car. Jason praying for her did make her feel a little better, though she still felt somewhat nervous. She pushed opened the front doors of the pharmacy trying to muster any courage she had inside of her, resolving herself to give it her all.

"You sure they haven't called your cell phone yet?"

"No Audrey, no one has called yet." Jason looked over at her and saw her shoulders slump. "But it's only been two days, sometimes these types of decisions can take time and they can still be interviewing others as well."

They were in the kitchen. Jason was washing the dishes and Audrey rinsed and dried them after he was finished.

"I guess you're right."

"You said you felt that the hiring manager liked you, right? I'm sure they'll call, just be patient."

When Audrey looked over into his eyes there were sparkles in hers. "Thanks Jason for being here for me. I really appreciate you." Her face was gentle and sincere. Jason's heart suddenly raced faster. He started washing the dishes again. What was wrong with him?

"You're welcome." He passed her the plate he'd just cleaned.

"I mean, you really didn't have to help me. You could've left me at the restaurant that night, but you didn't." Audrey paused before continuing. "You really are different from the other men whose main reason for helping me was only to use me. Thank you for your reason for helping me being about my soul and not about your gain."

Jason reflected on what she'd just said, sudden guilt creeping over him. He reaching out to Audrey was never entirely based on winning her soul, it was for his gain too and what he could get out of her. Really if he were to be honest with himself, that was the main reason. If Pastor James had never called him into his office that day, he would've never went to Lankford Avenue that night, especially putting into equation how much he didn't like outreaching. Suddenly he felt like Cash and the men who'd used Audrey. Although it wasn't for her body like them he was still using her in a different way.

"You ok over there?"

The sound of Audrey's voice snapped him from out of his thoughts. Jason realized he'd stopped washing the dishes. "Oh…yeah." He began cleaning them again and went to another topic not wanting to dwell on the guilt he felt. "How did you end up without a place to stay that night anyways?"

Audrey went quiet before answering. "Cash found out where I lived and he was trying to break in into my apartment. I ran away because I thought he might kill me if he got his hands on me."

Jason could read the fear on her face. "Do you know if he's still here in Tampa? How did he find you?" Jason felt himself getting angry. Cash needed to be put in prison for all of the horrible things he'd done to Audrey.

"I don't know how he found out I was in Tampa. But knowing his love for money and how he doesn't waste time when it comes to it, he probably left already after seeing that I ran." At least Audrey hoped so.

After waking up late in the middle of that night from the sounds of blaring thunder, Jason came into the kitchen to drink a glass of water. When he was done on his way passing the living room he saw a black figure sitting upright on the couch. Startled at first, he looked closer and discovered it was only Audrey.

"You almost gave me a heart attack." He let out a sigh of relief. "What are you doing out here anyways? Why aren't you sleeping in your room?"

"I don't like thunderstorms. It's been keeping me up all night." Audrey wrapped her arms around herself, looking like a frightened child. Jason could think of a probable reason for her not liking thunderstorms; her mom had overdosed during one.

"Well…maybe you should at least try going back to sleep again. Hopefully the rain will let up soon."

"No, it's ok." She shook her head. "Don't worry about me, you should go back to sleep so you won't be tired in the morning. You already work so hard for your church affairs."

Jason didn't want to leave her all alone in the dark, but there was no way he would invite her to sleep in his bed with him. He left and went back to his room.

Audrey balled herself on the couch and stared up at the ceiling.

It seemed like every time she tried to close her eyes images from her past would reappear.

Three minutes later Jason surprised her by returning to the living room with two covers and pillows in his arms.

"Here." He handed her a cover and a pillow. "I'll sleep on the other couch."

Audrey didn't reject his offer so Jason knew she must've been really shaken up. After they both got settled comfortably onto their couches Jason lay awake for a while. He felt grief for Audrey and everything she'd went through as a child all the way up to now. It made him begin to see how much he'd taken his blessings for granted.

Jason heard Audrey moving around on the other couch and she started making whimpering noises. He turned his head her way. Audrey looked like she was fighting someone in her sleep.

"No Cash please stop." She cried as if she were in pain.

"Audrey." Jason called out her name, but she still cried not hearing him.

"Audrey." He said louder.

Finally Audrey awoke from her nightmare, wide eyed like she'd just seen a ghost.

"Are you ok Audrey?"

Audrey nodded her head. "It's ok. I have those types of nightmares all of time. I should be used to them by now." Tears fell from her eyes and she wiped them away with the back of her hand. "It's no use, I won't be able to sleep tonight. You can go back in your room."

"No." Jason paused. "You can come over here and sleep with me." The words escaped his mouth before he even knew it. Jason couldn't believe he'd said the words he'd just did. He felt like he was becoming too comfortable with Audrey, but despite that he didn't want to see her suffer in any way and he couldn't help feeling that way. He was confident in the fact he didn't like Audrey, and that the only reason he felt the way he did was because of God. From Audrey being hesitant to come on the couch with him he knew she was just as surprised by his idea as well.

"Don't take it in the wrong way or anything. I just wanted for you to get a good night's rest is all, but if you don't want to its fine."

"No...I'll come over." Audrey stood up slowly and walked to the couch Jason lay on. For some reason she felt nervous. Could the reason Jason be being so nice to her was because he liked her? No, Jason had already said before he'd never be with someone who used to be a sleazy prostitute. Audrey needed to get rid of her silly thoughts, besides Audrey didn't like Jason either. She needed to be careful not to confuse her feelings of appreciation for Jason with feelings of affection.

Audrey lye down on the couch with Jason, letting there be as much space between them as possible. She didn't want Jason to get the notion she was coming on to him or anything. Because of her trying to create some distance between them Audrey felt her body began to slide from off of the edge of the sofa. She tried scooting back up again, but her body kept slipping down. All of a sudden

Audrey felt Jason's large hand press gently in the middle of her back and he drew her body into his.

"Are you trying to fall from off of the couch or something?" He said with his eyes still pressed together, looking as if he were about to doze off in any moment. "Just try going to sleep already, ok."

"Ok." Audrey said in a soft voice.

Her face was pressed against Jason's chest. He still had his arm around her. Lying with him she felt protected, and the nightmare she'd just experienced moments ago melted away. Audrey relaxed in his hold. She was becoming a pro on how to control her erupting emotions. Audrey shook her head to herself. Who was she trying to fool? Even now in his arms she felt all warm and bubbly inside. She figured it was about time for her to face it; she was falling in love with Jason.

Chapter 13

Audrey watched Jason as he peered at his cell phone like he'd done already for maybe the 100th time that day. The book he'd initially sat down to read was long forgotten, limp in his other hand. His attention was now avidly set on his cell phone. He looked at it with yearning eyes as if he were eager for someone to call him, more than likely that someone being Rebecca.

As she came to think of it Audrey hadn't heard Jason talk much about Rebecca since he playfully hugged her that night after finding Lulu. She wondered if anything had evolved between the two. Since admitting to herself that she had feelings for Jason a small part of her didn't want them to be romantically involved anymore, but the bigger part of her wanted his happiness no matter what. "Are you waiting on Rebecca to call you?" Audrey asked casually like she didn't care.

"No." Jason said. In actuality he was anticipating for the retail pharmacy she'd applied to to call his cell phone, but he wasn't going to let Audrey know that bit of information.

Jason went back to reading his book.

For a few seconds Audrey remained quiet as she scratched behind Lulu's ear. "By the way, have you attempted that hug on Rebecca yet?" She tried to be discreet with the use of her words, not wanting to come off as too nosy, and in turn giving away the feelings she possessed towards him.

"No I haven't. Actually ever since seeing her that day with you in the store I haven't seen her anymore."

"Really? But I thought you two were keeping in contact with one another."

"We were for about the first two weeks following that day, but then she suddenly stopped texting me back." Jason shrugged. From his nonchalant attitude it looked like he wasn't too upset about it. But still who was Rebecca, the want to be queen of England, to stand Jason up.

"Well it's her lost not yours." The words slipped from out of Audrey's mouth.

Jason stared at her for a moment with slightly wide eyes. Then he went back to reading his book again, with somewhat of a small smile lingering upon his lips.

"Why do you seem to be so interested about Rebecca and me all of a sudden?" He kept his eyes on the book in his hands, but she could feel his gaze through his peripheral vision.

Audrey squirmed inside. Was Jason already catching on that she had feelings for him? She didn't want him to know and for things to change between he and her. And she knew if he found out anyways he wouldn't like her. Audrey quickly thought up an excuse.

"I was only asking because I wanted to help you in any way that I can with winning her affections over. Remember when I told you that? I know all about what ladies want." Audrey said to him, hoping she sounded convincing enough.

Before Jason could say anything else to her his phone vibrated against the arm of the couch. He reached for it quickly and his book fell from out of his hand, but he answered the phone anyway like he didn't notice. After saying hello and listening to what the person on the other end had to say Jason looked over at Audrey with an expression she couldn't make out. Then he handed the phone to her.

"It's for you." He said.

Audrey took the phone in her shaky hand, as she did so feeling a bomb of nerves detonating inside the pit of her stomach. She knew it could only be one person. It was the manager from the pharmacy calling to tell her whether she'd gotten the job or not. She braced herself for the news, whether it be good or bad.

Jason watched Audrey as she spoke into the receiver. He could tell that she was nervous, and so was he, but he did his best to hide it from her. Audrey said "yes ma'am" then hung up the phone looking stiff in the face.

"So....what did she say?" Jason asked after Audrey didn't say anything.

Audrey looked down in her lap as if she could cry. "She said...she said I got the job!"

Later that day Jason cooked up a big meal for dinner to congratulate her success. Before helping themselves Jason prayed first as he always did. Audrey sunk her teeth into her food and complimented him on how delicious it tasted.

Jason smiled watching her do what he now referred to as her *"happy eating dance"* because she did it every time they ate dinner together. "So when do you start your new job?"

"Wednesday of next week." Audrey said grinning.

Audrey was so joyous. She couldn't stop smiling even as she ate her food, and Jason couldn't be happier for her. Finally Audrey was seeing she could do something else besides prostituting. Although it may have been a small step, it was a step nonetheless in Audrey realizing her potential that she could do whatever she put her mind to.

After a few minutes of eating Audrey put down her fork. "I've been thinking lately that I want to become saved. I want to give my life over to Jesus." She said with a solemn expression on her face. "I want to experience that freedom Jesus spoke about in the movie we watched. I want to be free from my past. And I want to get rid of the emptiness I feel inside and become the person God wants me to be."

"Well, that's great Audrey." Jason nodded surprised and also elated that she'd grown an aspiration to follow God and gain freedom for her past.

"But how do I become saved?" Audrey asked. "My dad told me once that there was a prayer people said when getting saved, but I can't remember the words."

"Well whatever they were you don't have to say those exact words to become saved." Jason sat more upright in his chair. Evangelism wasn't his strong suit, but words were suddenly coming to him on what to say. "Salvation is based on you having faith that Jesus dyed on the cross to take away your sins. It's about repenting and living a life that's pleasing to God, whatever words you decide to express that to Jesus when you give your life over to him is up to you, as long as afterwards your life begins to align with your confession."

"Do you mind assisting me in prayer? I like it when you pray. I can always feel the love you have for God whenever you do."

Suddenly Jason felt shy. Audrey's eyes were enlarged and filled with wonder like a small child's as she looked at him. Though he felt put on the spot how could Jason say no to that?

"Ok." Jason nodded and grabbed Audrey's hands in his. "Repeat after me." He closed his eyes, feeling a spirit of harmony and peace as he began to pray. "Lord I believe you sent Jesus to die on the cross for my sins. I know that I am a sinner in need of a savior. Lord make me new. I accept Jesus as Lord and savior over my life from here on out. I will give you the glory through all things and with your grace and provision over my life I will never be the same. In Jesus name I pray Amen."

"Amen." Audrey smiled after finishing repeating him.

And after that night Audrey wasn't ever the same. Something became awakened inside of her. She felt different after Jason had prayed for her, becoming eager to grow and learn more about God.

She'd asked to borrow Jason's Bible and for hours on end would be in her room reading it, experiencing a divine joy she'd never known before when doing so. When there were something's she didn't understand she would go and ask Jason about it. Whatever he was doing at the moment he would set it aside and always be willing to try to help her understand whatever scripture she was having difficulty to comprehend. Jason was very skilled when it came to teaching her the Word, though it didn't surprise her. He was good at everything.

The more she drew closer to God, the more she began to know for sure she was falling in love with Jason. In the beginning stages of discovering her feelings for him she tried to fight it. At first she thought how could she be so sure it was love. She didn't think she knew what love was, but she knew she'd never experienced the same feelings she had for Jason for another man before. Being around him brought inner joy to her being, just like she got whenever reading the Word. But even though she felt this way she thought it was best to keep it to herself. For the remaining time she had to stay with him she wanted things to remain the way they were, by just simply enjoying their friendship. And part of her felt afraid to hear his reply if she ever did confess her feelings to him, she knew Jason wouldn't feel the same way as she did and reject her.

Audrey walked down the street after taking the bus home from work. It was her first day and thankfully everything seemed to be going smoothly so far, though she couldn't say she did any real work that day. The entire first of her day consisted of her completing a virtual orientation on an outdated computer in a freezing room in the back of the pharmacy. But so far the coworkers she was scheduled to work with were nice so that was a bonus.

She unlocked the door with the spare key Jason had entrusted her with having her mind already set on going to her room. Although she'd sat down all day for some reason she felt tired and wanted to take a nap.

When she got to the living room there stood a half-naked Jason in front of her. The only thing covering him being a towel wrapped around his waist. Her mouth dropped and so did her purse in her right hand. Jason had just noticed she was even there because his back was turned. He swung around to face her and his eyes became big as he placed his arms over his chest, which was much toner than what Audrey thought, revealing he had six pack abs. He then turned around running down the hallway, in the process hitting his toe on the corner. Yelling in pain he continued to hop down the hallway on one foot. After getting over the initial shock Audrey couldn't help but to give out a laugh.

When Jason was done dressing himself he came back into the living room barely being able to look at her.

"I thought you worked until later today. I would've come to pick you up." He rubbed the back of his neck looking down at the floor.

"I had got the times mixed up with the day that I work on Thursday." Audrey said.

"Oh, ok. Well…how was your first day at work?" He coughed.

"It was good. I met some of the people I'm going to be working shifts with and they all seem pretty nice."

"That's really good. I'm glad that you are liking it so far." Jason nodded and then remained quiet.

The silence became awkward which each second that passed.

"Well, you are much toner than what you appear clothed." Audrey smiled thinking it would break the ice. Instead Jason looked even more embarrassed.

Later that day Audrey noticed Jason didn't come out of his office since briefly talking with him earlier. Hoping he wasn't mad at her regarding her statement, which she only meant to be as a joke to lighten the mood, she went to his office and knocked on his door.

"Come in." He called out.

She entered his office and saw him hunched over some papers on his desk. He was rubbing his temples as if he was stressed out about something.

"I haven't heard from you since earlier, just making sure you're ok." Audrey said in a timid tone.

"I'm ok, thanks." Jason focused on the papers in front of him, not bothering to look her way.

Figuring she must've made him upset earlier she turned to leave his office, but then turned around again to face him. "Are you sure you're ok?"

Jason finally looked up at her, like he'd just snapped back to reality. "Yeah I'm good." He nodded his head sincerely. "It's just that I'm looking over the budget for the youth ministry and it's turning out to be a time-consuming task. I'm trying to figure out how the budget is going to cover the cost of all of the events planned for this year, while at the same time brainstorming some fundraiser ideas to raise money."

"Oh." Audrey said feeling relieved he wasn't upset with her.

"How about I give you a hand?" She walked towards him. Audrey saw the looked of astonishment on his face from her offer. "What?" She shrugged. "I know all about budgeting. I used to could get by a whole week with only ten dollars on hand. Out of those ten dollars I could buy a whole week's worth of grocery, even if it was mainly noodles, and still have some money left over to get Lulu her cat food."

The next thirty minutes turned to hours as Audrey went over the papers with Jason and gave him advice concerning cheaper routes to take so that the budget could cover the total cost of things. She also shared great fundraising ideas to him he'd never thought of, such as yard sales, street carnivals and hosting cook offs to raise money. When she gave her ideas she seemed really passionate about it. Her new love for God and ministry Jason admitted were admirable. The whole time she talked he could see the enthusiasm in her eyes.

Time had escaped them. After having spent several hours strategizing and planning the both of them ended up dozing off to sleep. Audrey awoke in the middle of the night with her face pressed against the desk with Jason's face right in front of hers. He was sleeping, looking like an angel as he did so. For a moment she just watched him as he slept, taking in the peace she felt. Then she found a blanket to cover him with not wanting to wake him from his tranquil sleep. Before leaving to go to her room she wrote down some more ideas and tided up Jason's desk area for him.

Jason went to Audrey's door to let her know dinner was ready. As he was about to knock on it he heard her singing on the other end causing his hand to stop in midair. She was singing praises to God. Her voice was beautiful. Not overly powerful, but sweet and humble. As he listened to her sing he leaned his head on her door and closed his eyes. Her song and the way she sang it sent soothing chills through his body. She sung to Him thanking Him for giving her another chance, thanking Him for His never failing love and mercies. He smiled, happy that Audrey was finding her joy in God.

Before they ate dinner this time Audrey had prayed and when she opened her eyes after she'd finished she saw Jason smiling at her.

Audrey's heart beat faster from his warmhearted smile. To distract herself from the way she was feeling she took a bite of her serving. "Good as always." She complimented him.

"Thank you." Jason said to her. "Since you've been working for over a month now I think it's a good time for you to come to church this Sunday and give your testimony."

"Ok." Audrey smiled, but the thought of her having to give her testimony now bringing her discomfort.

Jason picked up the sudden change in her mood after he'd brought the testimony up. Audrey didn't say much of anything as she slowly ate the rest of her food in silence. At first he tried to ignore it because he needed for her to give her testimony. Mr. Thomson was gaining more favor at the church and Jason knew that if his plan with Audrey didn't fall through he was going to lose the chance of grabbing the position to him or someone else. But as the silence grew he couldn't take it anymore.

"What's the matter?" He asked her.

"It's just...it's just that I don't want to have to tell everyone about my past. I'm afraid people may look at me like I'm still dirty."

"No Audrey that's not true. You're testimony could help someone else who may be going through a similar situation or if they know someone who is." Jason said trying to convince her not to back out.

Audrey could see how much Jason really wanted her to give her testimony. "Ok, fine. I'll do it for you. I mean you have helped me without asking anything in return." She said attempting to tame back her fear.

Although Jason felt bad about it this had to be done. It wasn't like he was committing a sin like the others who'd used her before did. Jason had helped her in many ways, it was about time he be rewarded for it.

Jason parked his car in the front of his church on Sunday morning. He looked to his right to find Audrey appearing ill in the face. Last night Jason couldn't sleep properly, he knew it was because of his conscious and how he felt like he was acting like the other men who'd used Audrey, no matter how much he tried to convince himself that he wasn't like them.

"Are you ok?" She hadn't said anything for the whole ride there.

Audrey nodded because she couldn't open her mouth to get anything to come out of it. Looking at his church made her anxiety worsen. The church building was large, almost the size of a mega church. No wonder how Jason was able to make such decent amount of money to live the way he did. She was expecting a small church, but the size of this one was intimidating. How was she going to stand up there in front of everyone and divulge to them her darkest memories? Audrey tried to breathe before the fear she felt rising suffocated her.

Seeing her go through such emotional affliction on the cause of him was too much for Jason to stomach anymore. Audrey had already gone through so much. He didn't want to add on more burdens to her list due to his selfish ambition. He felt the guilt more than ever now, and this time he wasn't going to try to fight it. He felt ashamed. It had become more about her helping him getting the position of executive pastor and less about her soul. Maybe Pastor James was right about him. Maybe he wasn't cut out to be a pastor.

"Listen Audrey, I wasn't completely honest with you from the beginning." Now Jason felt himself getting nervous as he prepared himself to tell her the full truth. "When I came to witness to you that night it was not based solely on winning your soul. Matter of fact the reason I decided to help you was based on something else. I helped you because I wanted to elevate from being a minister at my church to becoming the executive pastor. My head pastor told me I wasn't friendly or evangelical enough and in order for me to even be considered for the title I would have to start proving myself in that area, so that's when I came up with the bright idea of going to Lankford Avenue to win a soul to prove to him that I could be evangelical."

Audrey remained quiet, taking in what he'd told her. She didn't know how she should feel about his confession. Considering his reason people had used her for things much far worse. All she had was one question for him.

"How about now, has the reason changed? Do you have some care in your heart for me now?"

Jason paused before answering, slightly taken off guard from her straightforward question. "I guess you could say so."

"It's a yes or a no question."

"Well yes…yes I've come to care for you… as a brother would his annoying sister." Jason chuckled then looked into her eyes with sincerity. "And that's why I told you the truth. I don't want you going up there anymore if you don't want to. I don't want to be like the other men in your life who only helped you to get something out of you."

Jason turned the keys in the ignition. "I'm going to take you back home."

"No…it's ok. I would like to do this for you…and for me."

"Are you sure Audrey? I don't want you going up there because you feel pressured. I'm really ok with you not going up there anymore."

"Yes, I'm sure. I want to do this."

Jason led her inside of the church. As they walked to the front to sit down many people eyed them down. Jason knew the looks were more so out of curiosity seeing he had never brought anyone to church before and that his guest being a woman made it the more mysterious to them.

He sat down next to her and leaned over to her side. "When the time comes for the testimonies and if you don't feel like doing it then don't do it, okay."

Audrey nodded her head trying to come off as strong in front of Jason as she could. On the inside she felt afraid out of her mind. But because Jason was truthful to her and was so adamant about her not doing it made her want to do it even more for him. Audrey could see he had developed some care for her. He was the first person in a long time to ever show such a sincere concern for her and she appreciated it. Seeing as how kind he'd been to her over the course of these four months she wanted to do something nice for him in return.

The worship service begun and it was so good it made Audrey get to her feet and join in on the praise. For a brief second she forgot about everything until an older gentleman came up and asked if anyone in the congregation had a testimony to share.

Audrey stood up and walked to the front to get it over with. Good thing she was already seated in the front because her legs shook so bad she didn't think she could walk much further. The man extended his arm and she took the microphone from his hand. She looked into the crowd to see many faces of different backgrounds staring back at her. Her eyes met Jason who gave her an encouraging smile.

"Hello everyone, my name is Audrey." She started and then took a mini breath to calm herself. "I used to be a prostitute."

Jason clutched his hand closed, his heart beating ferociously inside of his chest. He didn't know that watching Audrey give her testimony would make him feel like it was him up there instead. He did a prayer that God would get the glory out of Audrey's testimony and not himself, and that Audrey would be able to get through it, because right now he could see the nervousness all over her. Everyone in the crowd remained quiet, attentive on what else she had to say.

"When I was eleven-years-old I was raped by my step father, my mother died when I was twelve and the abuse worsened after that. To escape from the abuse I ran away at the age of fifteen, but I ran right into the arms of a pimp. For the next two years I went through the worse kind of treatment imaginable. He forced me to become a prostitute and he played mind games with me. I took the role of a prostitute hating it, but as time passed I became accustomed to it, thinking that it was my only hand in life and that I had no way out. I tried not to lose what was left of me, but the misery took hold of me of what I'd become. When I looked in the mirror, I hated the person staring back at me." Audrey paused as tears swelled in her eyes.

"But God sent a person in my life. This person showed me the beauty of serving God and the beauty of God's mercy. I gave my life over to Jesus by seeing this person live out what he professed to believe in. God gave me another chance and I'm just so thankful.

After all of the shameful things that I've done in my life God still welcomed me with arms wide open. And I just want to thank Him." Audrey cried as the tears fell from her eyes. "And I want to thank Jason Goodman for being the person God used to show me His love. He encouraged me that God is able to save any soul, no matter how wretched. Thank you Jason." She looked his way with such gratitude causing his eyes to moisten. Jason held back his tears.

"You don't know how much you've changed my life." Audrey closed her eyes and wept. She covered her face with her arm and stood speechless.

People stood up and started clapping. Many shouted "Amen".

After service was over countless of people approached Audrey and Jason telling her how moving her story was. Audrey felt like she was introduced to at least half of the church by the time it was done and over with. They were all kind and welcoming people. She left church that day feeling refreshed and overjoyed.

Chapter 14

"So what did she want from you?" Jason said grabbing the phone from her after Audrey was finished.

He was curious to know why Cindy had called his cell phone asking if he knew how she could contact Audrey. Cindy hadn't called him in ages. Though just months ago his feelings concerning her were not the best, now he had no ill feelings towards her. Jason understood that something's in life were just not meant to be, and there was no needing to dwell on a past that couldn't be changed. Well—that's how he felt for the moment at least.

"She wanted to know if I'd like to volunteer with her on some project she's a part of. We are meeting at the church tomorrow after

Bible study ends."

The following night after Bible study was over Jason showed Audrey to the conference room Cindy told her she'd be meeting her at. Cindy was already sitting at the table when they entered the room. When she saw them she gave the both of them a friendly smile.

"Hi, thank you for meeting me Audrey." She then looked over at Jason. "I won't keep her for too long."

"Oh, it's no problem. You two chat for as long as you need to. I have something's to finish up before leaving anyways." Jason said. "By the way it's nice seeing you Cindy."

"And you too." Cindy said to Jason before he left them to talk alone.

"It's nice to official sit down to meet you." Cindy smiled at her.

"It's nice meeting you too."

"I want to start off by saying your story is so heart moving and demonstrates the power of God's redemption so beautifully."

"Thank you." Audrey said, thinking that Cindy so far seemed like a genuinely nice person.

"No, thank you for sharing it with us Audrey, I know that it helped a lot of people."

At first they talked for a while getting to know each other personally. From the way Cindy spoke so familiar with her made Audrey feel like there was a sister bond going on. She made Audrey feel comfortable to open up to her.

"So I called you here because I wanted to talk with you about a women's ministry I'm involved with called *Hope for Tomorrow*. We do lots of outreaching to women on the streets, where we provide assistance to those who are homeless, on drugs or who need help in any way to get their life back on track. Our women's group was actually just talking recently about us needing to go even further this year to reach the lost. Would you be interested in joining our ministry? I think you would have so much to offer."

"Well sure, but what is it that I'd need to do?" Audrey didn't think she'd have many skills to offer.

"Simply giving your input would be a great start to help us. Do you know of anyone who would be in need of assistance?"

Audrey could think of only one person, Trina, and that was even if she'd accept any of their help. Hopefully she wasn't dead by now from her addiction to drugs. Part of her still felt betrayed that Trina had snitched her whereabouts to Cash, but it was the past and she'd just read a scripture on forgiving others.

On the way driving home Audrey told Jason what their meeting was about and he responded positive telling her he thought it was a great idea.

"Just be sure when you do go over to Trina's place to have Cindy or one of the other women to go with you. Although we do forgive people she still can't be trusted just yet. Trust has to be earned."

"You're right." Audrey looked over at him. "By the way I was meaning to tell you I think you'd be a great executive pastor. And just because you don't hold the title doesn't mean you can't perform as one. You don't need a title to help and love on people."

Her words sparked a warm feeling inside of him. Later that night he stayed up thinking about her statement. Audrey was right. He didn't need a title when it came to treating people with love as Jesus did.

The sun was blazing on them outside like it had a grudge to pick with the world as people lined up to get their share of the free food. Audrey wiped the sweat that'd formed on her forehead as she scooped the green beans on the foam plate to serve the next person. Jason was volunteering to outreach that day with his church in the projects and had invited Audrey to come along with him. Right now he was loading boxes of canned food in somebody's car.

"Thank you for coming out today." David, who Audrey had discovered was Cindy's husband and also Jason's older brother, turned over to her and smiled. They kind of looked alike with the shape of their square faces. He was also helping to serve by putting the portions of rice on people's platters in line beside her.

"It's no problem." Audrey said to him. "After all God has done for me it's only right that I give back. I enjoy doing things like this."

David looked over in the distance to where Jason was. "You know you coming into my brother's life has changed him tremendously. This is his first time ever participating in an outreach event."

"Really?" Audrey said surprised.

"Yes. You know Jason used to be extremely shy when we were kids, not wanting to interact with people much. He talked so rarely that the doctor's thought he had a speaking problem or something, but he got much better as he grew older. But he's so different now, in a good way. In fact he even seems more upbeat. I know it must have something to do with him meeting you."

Audrey looked down feeling her cheeks warm. Could it be possible that she was held at such a high esteem in Jason's life?

"After our mom's passing when we were kids this is the first time I've seen him actually look happy."

This was Audrey's first time hearing about Jason's mom. "Your mom passed?"

"Yeah, I'm not surprised Jason didn't tell you. It's something he doesn't like to talk about. He's a person who still keeps a lot to himself, but I know he's hurting inside." David said with sorrow in his eyes. "But Jason gets it from our father. I think the both of them put so much energy into their work to forget their pain. After my mom passed away my father started working himself even harder, as if he didn't already do enough being the head pastor over the church."

"What? Jason's father, I mean you guy's father is the Head Pastor—Pastor James?"

"Yeah...he didn't tell you that either?"

"No. Jason always refers to him as his pastor, not his father."

David stayed quiet for a while as if he was thinking something over, looking slightly saddened while doing so.

"Well, he's making steps. I hope you'll continue being a positive influence in his life. He's been such a lonely person for so long." David said.

As the sun began to set everybody pitched in to break down the tables and clean up the area. Audrey saw an older lady approach Jason thanking him for all he and everyone else had done that day. Even where Audrey stood she could see Jason's eyes water as he told the lady "You're welcome." She noticed now that Jason was like a teddy bear inside. Although he appeared strong and resolute on the outside, he went through things as well though trying to keep it in.

"Are you still enjoying working at the pharmacy?" Jason asked Audrey over dinner the next day.

"Yeah I am. I think I'm catching onto things pretty quick. My coworkers are really nice too, one is even a Christian, but I think my supervisor doesn't like it when I try to talk people out of buying cigarettes or when I say things to them like "are you sure you want to pollute your body with that stuff and knock years off of your precious life?""

Jason laughed. "That sounds like something I would do."

"Well I did learn from the best." Audrey chuckled.

Over the next few minutes Audrey contemplated in her head whether or not should she bring up what David had revealed to her, it had been on her mind since last night. After trying to keep it in she couldn't tame it any longer. The curiosity was burning her all up inside.

"Why didn't you tell me your father was Pastor James?"

Jason stopped eating and placed down his fork. "Well, I didn't think it was such a big deal."

"Why don't you acknowledge him as your father?"

"Because I see him as a pastor as well."

"What about your mom? Why didn't you tell me she passed away? I told you all there is to know about my life."

"Just because you told me about your life doesn't mean I have to tell you about mine." Jason said getting aggravated. "And who told you this anyways? Was it David?"

"Yes, it was David. And I'm sorry if me bringing it up is upsetting you, but you should know you can talk with me about anything."

"And why would I want to do that huh?" Jason stood from his chair. "I'm going in my office to finish some work."

Audrey sat silent. She didn't know her question would cause Jason to become so unsettled. There must've been something he was very hurt about like his brother had said. Even still she thought that maybe he would've opened up to her considering they had formed some kind of friendship. Or maybe that friendship was one-sided, all in Audrey's head. Maybe David was wrong about Jason being different because of her.

Audrey got her work clothes prepared for tomorrow, about to ready herself for bed after not hearing a word from Jason for the rest of that night. Then she heard a small knock on her door.

"Come in." She said in a quiet tone.

Jason came in looking down at the floor. "I'm sorry how I reacted earlier."

"It's ok. I shouldn't have butted in."

For a moment Jason remained quiet, looking like a lost child. "My mother died in a horrible car accident when I was seven."

Audrey drew in a breath. "I'm so sorry Jason." She said with sadness.

Jason shuffled his feet from side to side. "The reason why I don't call my father, father is because as a young child I never really saw him much as a father figure. He always put his pastoral duties first. This caused my mother to resent him and eventually they separated. They didn't divorce due to how it would look bad to the church, but after they separated I never saw much of my mother anymore. Due to her suffering from depression and a slew of other mental issues my dad kept my brother and I. But at whatever chance she got she would always have David over to her house, and not me. I remember once she told me I was too much like my father, I was such a "serious kid" as she put it. I think she liked David more because he was always happy and friendly with everyone. My dad would pay me no attention; he'd either be in his office working or away on pastoral duties. I became jealous of David because my mother loved him more than me and he would always get what I wanted...including Cindy." Jason paused.

"I remember I was feeling extremely lonely this one particular day as I looked out of the window sitting in the living room by myself. My dad was in his office providing some counsel to someone when his daughter walked up to me. The thing I noticed first about her was how pretty she was. She looked at me with her big brown eyes and a wide smile."

"What are you doing sitting here all alone?" She says to me.

I just look at her because I'm too shy to say anything back.

"Do you have any toys we can play with?" She asked.

I shake my head no and she looks at me like I'm crazy.

"What kid doesn't have any toys?"

She then digs in her pocket and pulls out two small racecar toys.

"I got these from my brother, but you can have one."

"Since her dad would come over a lot to visit mine, after that day Cindy and I became best friends. She was actually the only friend I had, but as we grew up she started taking an interest in David more. I'm not certain if Cindy knew, but I'm pretty sure David knew my feelings for her because he'd always tease me about her. But he ignored my feelings regarding her. The next thing I knew they were getting married and I was the best man at their wedding. But of course I let my feelings go of what I had for her. It was just another instance, as always, where David got what he wanted."

"But you know he loves you right?" Audrey said, sensing bitterness from Jason's tone. "When I talked to him the other day I could tell that he does."

"You know, I'm not at all surprised that you'd say that. David has a way of easily winning people over."

"But he hasn't won me over. There's no other person in this world that I admire and look up to more than I do to you. I'm so grateful for you."

Jason looked into her eyes and he could tell that Audrey sincerely meant what she'd just said. He felt his heart dance a ferocious beat as her eyes sparkled across the room. Suddenly he felt like all the oxygen was stuck in the middle of his throat.

"Well, I'll be heading off to bed now so you can get yourself some rest for work tomorrow. Goodnight." He quickly left her room.

Audrey closed her legs tight together, trying to hold her urgent need to go to the ladies restroom to empty her bladder. She was at Bible study and the speaker was saying some really great things she didn't want to miss out on. She wanted to continue to listen and take notes. Jason was off somewhere in the church, as he'd told her to do ministry work, so she couldn't use him to take notes for her. And plus her being seated right in the middle of the row she didn't want to walk in front of people interrupting them from paying attention from the lesson as well. She stayed seated for a few minutes longer as she scribbled down notes, but couldn't hold it in any longer. She stood making her way down the row as she excused herself and apologized to those whom she had to walk in front of, luckily they all seemed understanding.

Making her way down the empty hallway to the ladies room Audrey spotted two people hugged up in a corner further down. At first she thought nothing of it and kept walking, but then she looked again because she thought it was something familiar about the taller figure. To her discernment and great surprise she was right. That taller person was Jason, but that wasn't the only thing that surprised her. The other person he was hugging up with was Cindy! And they seemed mighty comfortable while cozied up together too. She held back her rage she harvested for the both of them and went into the restroom. When she came back out into the hallway they were gone. The rest of the Bible study she couldn't even concentrate any longer on the message, not believing she was fooled by them. Here she was thinking they were the most nicest and righteous people she'd ever met, but in reality they were sneaking around committing adultery.

Audrey washed a plate and handed it to him forcefully. She seemed angry. Jason had noticed she seemed angry since dinner. She ate silently throughout the meal. Even when Jason had tried to create a conversation with her she wouldn't respond back to him and she kept giving him mean glares. Her sudden hostility towards him was confusing.

"Are you alright Audrey?" He said attempting to break the silence.

"Yes, I'm totally fine." She scrubbed harder on the plate she was washing.

"You don't seem fine to me."

Audrey stopped washing the plate and took a heavy breath.

"I…I just thought you were different is all."

"I am different." Jason said confused. "Didn't you even say so yourself?"

"Well, that was before…"

"Before what?"

"Before I saw you hugged up all over Cindy is what." Audrey blurted it out, feeling enraged all over again like when she felt when seeing them intertwined together.

For a moment it took Jason a while to figure out what she was talking about until he remembered last night. "You must be talking about during Bible study yesterday. I can assure you that that hug meant nothing. I don't have any feelings for her anymore whatsoever."

"Are you sure about that?" Audrey said not fully being convinced. "So why were you two hugging then?"

"She told me she's been having miscarriage signs for the last couple of days. She confessed to me that they'd had a miscarriage before that they'd kept a secret from the church so she's pretty familiar of the signs. They are seeing their doctor tomorrow. She asked me to pray for her and I did. As I prayed she got emotional and hugged me so I hugged her back as a means to comfort her, and that was the only reason."

Audrey put her head down. After hearing his reason, feeling ashamed of herself for misunderstanding things and at the same time hoping everything would be alright with Cindy and her baby.

"I'm sorry. I feel so bad for misjudging you two." She said to

Jason.

"It's ok." He said.

For the rest of the time they cleaned the dishes Audrey didn't say anything else. Jason could tell she was still beating herself up inside for her accusatory behavior. To make light of the situation Jason gently grabbed her by her arm. Audrey looked up at him clearly taken back.

"And don't worry I didn't give her one of these hugs." Jason put his arms around Audrey, his hands rested on her back.

At first Jason was planning for the hug to be just another joke, where he would laugh afterwards like the first time. But instead when Audrey surprisingly placed her arms atop his shoulders a jolt surged in his body. He became hot all over and couldn't pull away from her embrace. He wanted to rub his hands down her back and continue to take in her light sweet scent. Right now while holding her in his arms Jason was being brought to a level of bliss he'd never known before. Jason felt his body slipping, slipping away from his control. Then he thought about Jesus. As if some sense had been suddenly knocked into him Jason pulled away from her.

Jason looked into Audrey's eyes. If she wasn't mistaken she could've sworn she saw a hint of desire, but not only was there desire in them but fear too. She wasn't sure because as soon as he looked at her his cell phone rang.

He grabbed his phone and checked who was calling. "I have to take this. I'll probably be in my office for the rest of the night." He said before leaving.

Jason was normal to Audrey the days after. She concluded Jason had only acted the way he did towards her because he was uncomfortable with her. More than likely she was just imaging things when she was looking into his eyes, seeing only what she wanted to see. There was no way Jason would want someone like her. She was too tainted for him to desire her. Audrey couldn't allow her hopes to get up high again. She would have to do better at keeping her emotions balanced so she wouldn't be disappointed with her wishful thinking.

"Jason what made you want to become a doctor?" Audrey asked him one day after thinking long and hard about her future. She knew she wasn't staying with Jason forever. The months were steadily becoming shorter, so she knew she needed to think about her ability to remain stable when it came to providing for herself. She was sure she'd never go back to prostitution, even if she had to stay on the streets. She'd experienced too much joy and freedom being away from Lankford Avenue. Going back was not an option for her. And although she liked her job at the pharmacy it wasn't a career where she made a substantial amount of income to survive comfortably.

"I don't know. I just naturally did. Why?"

"I don't know what it is I want to be in life."

"Well, maybe you can start volunteering more at the church in different areas. Maybe then you will find something that you really like."

Audrey thought about it. What Jason suggested seemed like a good idea.

The next few weeks Audrey found a sense of belonging volunteering at the church, helping in whatever way that she could. She particularly discovered that she liked volunteering in the teen's ministry the most of all, where she could teach and mentor young girls. She loved to be able to offer them life lessons while they were yet young because it could save them from a lot of future mistakes and hurts such as Audrey had experienced. She felt that if she could touch just one it would all be worth it. The relationships she was developing with the girls were becoming stronger each time she mentored them, each one of them becoming to have a place in her heart.

During a Sunday service Audrey enlisted to fill in for one of the greeters who'd fell ill and couldn't show up that day. Justin, who was also a pupil of Jason's came up to her and smiled shyly. "Hello Ms. Audrey. It's nice seeing you today." He shook her hand nervously. "And thank you for the advice you gave me yesterday, it was very helpful." Before walking off he almost stumbled on his feet. Audrey pretended like she didn't notice when he glanced back at her embarrassed. It wasn't until he was out of sight that she giggled.

"It looks like someone is making a big hit with the youth. Every youth that comes in here speaks and smiles to you." Jason appeared from behind her.

"It's because they need someone to talk to about their issues, someone who will be honest with them and help them along the way."

"You seem to like this teaching thing a lot." Jason said, surprised by her sound words.

"I do." Audrey grinned. "You know he kind of reminds me of you, always so neat and proper. No wonder why you said he was drawn to you."

"Who? Justin?"

"Yeah. And he looks like he could use a friend. He's so to himself all of the time."

Now that Jason pondered on it, he did always see Justin alone.

A high school girl walked past them without so much as saying a word. She kept her gaze straight ahead like they weren't even there.

"Gabby, where are you going off to again?" Audrey asked her.

Gabby looked at Audrey with disdain. "I was going out for some fresh air." She rolled her neck as she said it.

"Really?" Audrey folded her arms. "While church is still going on, no you won't. You go back inside the service and listen to the Word. This is my fourth time seeing you roaming about. I don't want to see you out here again ok?"

Jason could see the want to protest written all over Gabby's face, but Audrey gave her such a rigid glare that made her shut up and listen. Seeing Audrey in her teacher mode was a sight to witness. He could tell that Audrey had found her niche.

"Yeah...ok." Gabby said with an attitude.

"I'll see you next Tuesday during girls Bible study, right?"

"I guess." Gabby walked off evidently angry and upset, even rolling her eyes at Audrey before she went back inside of the service.

"She's always been the one to be disrespectful." Jason shook his head remembering the time he had to break up a fight with her and another girl that she'd started.

"Although I've had my share of troubles with her so far, that's the exact reason why we can't give up on her. People are not already going to be cleaned up. You have to help them see the right way, like you did for me."

Jason blinked his eyes baffled due to her remark.

Did Audrey just school him?

He stared at her amazed by her growth and knowledge.

"I have to admit I can't believe I would've ever been able to learn anything from you." He told her.

"Well, thank you." Audrey began to smile, but then she stopped thinking over his comment some more. "Is that a compliment or an insult?"

"It's a compliment." Jason chuckled.

"Thanks Jason, that means a lot to me coming from you." Audrey said as she reached out and tapped him on his arm.

The place she touched him warmed his whole arm and Jason's body stiffened. They were the only ones by the entrance and she had that sparkle in her eyes again. Lately Jason didn't like how he was feeling when he would come around Audrey. He felt like he wanted to be near her all of the time and to take in her presence. Sometimes he would even think about her out of nowhere when she would be at work. He would count down the minutes waiting for her to come home so he could ask her how her day was. There was something really strange going on with him that he had to fix regarding his thoughts concerning her.

Audrey smiled merrily, appearing serene as she did so. He noticed Audrey had a golden glow to her skin. "You're not wearing any of that dark makeup anymore." He said.

"I'm actually not wearing any makeup at all."

"It looks nice." The words came out of his mouth by their own will. He could tell from the expression on Audrey's face that she was surprised by his compliment. Jason pushed his hands in his pockets and gave a small cough looking down at the floor. "Well, I'm just saying, it looks better than that gothic look you had going on."

Audrey pushed a strand of loose hair behind her ear. "Well, thank you." Part of Audrey wanted to get her hopes up high again, but the other part said that Jason only saw her as a friend. She couldn't let his nice words make her believe he may have liked her. "You just now noticing I stopped wearing makeup? I've been going without it for almost a month now."

Before Jason could answer to say what he was about to say his eyes became focused on whoever was coming up from behind Audrey through the entryway. His eyes grew large as if he were seeing a dead man walking.

Audrey turned around to see who he was gawking at.

The duchess came in with her head held high, already zeroing her eyes in on Jason with a flirty smile. When her eyes flickered over to Audrey her smile immediately vanished. Her face became distorted like a vicious K9, it was clear she had a bone to pick with Audrey and that she was now prepared for an all-out war.

Chapter 15

Since that fateful day of the duchess's return Audrey had become a wall to Jason. The duchess—Audrey meant Rebecca had joined the church and was wrapping Jason right around her little finger. It wasn't her intent to participate with Rebecca in this game of war. Audrey knew that even if she would that she'd come out with the shorter end. As long as Rebecca sincerely liked Jason and treated him with the respect he deserved she would gladly cheer on their relationship.

Jason didn't say that they'd officially started dating, but he would go out and say he was meeting with her over lunch almost every other day out of the week. Due to this reason Jason never made dinner anymore. When he ignored her, it hurt her, and when he was gone, she would miss him. Audrey knew she shouldn't feel the way she did, but she just couldn't help it.

"Are you ok Ms. Audrey?" Justin asked her.

Audrey snapped out of her daze, just noticing Justin was talking to her.

"Oh, I'm fine." Audrey said as she continued to neatly place each book back onto the second row of the bookshelf. She had volunteered today to help Justin alphabetize the books in the children's church classroom. They were also sorting out the ones that were ripped and colored on the inside. Finally they were almost done with row number two after an hour and a half of checking each and every book.

"Ok." He went quiet and put his head down, scanning through the pages of the book in his hands.

Sensing that there was something on his mind Audrey stopped what she was doing and turned her attention to him. Besides she shouldn't waste her time dwelling on Jason, and how he was making her feel like she was invisible lately. Thinking about it only made her feel more dejected.

"So how has everything been going with you Justin?" She attempted to create some conversation.

Justin slowly looked over to her and then back down at his book again. It took a moment before he said anything else. "You know the advice I asked you about last time?"

"Yes." Audrey nodded.

"Well…it's not working. At first I thought I could talk to her, but I get nervous every time I get around her."

Audrey thought about when she first discovered her feelings for Jason were developing, and how her heart would beat like rumbling drums whenever he'd come near her. Thinking about it almost made her smile. "That's a normal thing to feel when you're around the person you really like, but as you spend more time with this person you'll get better with how to convey your feelings to her."

"You think so?" Justin asked her, looking unconfident in himself.

Although he was nineteen he still looked like a freshman just entering into high school with his baby smooth almond skin. He was very tall for his age, taller than Audrey and almost the same height as Jason. Looking at him and how serious he was reminded Audrey so much of him. Their appearance was somewhat different however, Justin had more of an oval face and his eyes were rounder than Jason's.

"Yeah, I do. And I think whoever this young lady is will come to realize what a fine gentlemen you are. I'm sure the girls you're age find you very attractive, you are a handsome young man."

Justin looked away shyly. "Thank you." He gave a small smile.

"By the way, is this girl a Christian?"

"Yes she is. She loves God tremendously."

"Well that's good. She sounds like a great person already."

"I think she is." Justin nodded. "I want to thank you for taking the time out to help me with this project today. I usually am always given the task of doing this alone every year."

"Wow, you do all this by yourself? These are a lot of books to sort through even for two people, let alone one person."

"I know, but sometimes volunteers can be hard to come by these days." Justin put down the book in his hand. "I know we aren't going to get everything done today. Since we are halfway done, we can stop now and finish up next week."

"Ok." Audrey stood to stretch. She was so happy to hear Justin say those words. Her fingers were becoming numb and they tingled due to a few paper cuts she'd accumulated while flipping through the pages of the books.

Justin rubbed his hand on the back of his head and let out a light cough. "As a thank you gesture, can I take you out to eat somewhere?"

"Sure, thank you!" Audrey responded immediately. She hadn't ate anything all day and she knew Jason wasn't going to cook dinner…seeing if he was home anyways and not out with Rebecca.

"Do you like it?" Justin chuckled as he watched Audrey chew down a huge mouthful she'd just taken out of her burrito.

Audrey nodded and swallowed before answering. "Yes, it's delicious!" She giggled, knowing she probably looked like a greedy monster in front of him. "I've never tried authentic Mexican food before."

"Yeah, well you've missed out for too long. This is my favorite place to come eat."

"Do you come here a lot with your friends?"

"Nah." Justin shook his head. "I'm too busy for friends." Justin smiled, but she could see the loneliness in his eyes when he said it. She'd experienced that same loneliness before.

"I didn't have many friends either growing up." She said not wanting to make him feel embarrassed for not having any friends. It wasn't her intent to get on this subject anyhow, she was only making conversation. Now she felt sorry for even bringing it up.

Justin's eyes fell down to his plate and he didn't say anything for a long time. Audrey could see he was hesitant to divulge to her what was on his mind. "Yeah it's not really popular to be saved in college, not that it wasn't much easier when I was in high school either. But now I'm experiencing the pressure more than ever to conform."

Audrey could see that this was a topic that had been heavy on his chest for some time, because after he said it she saw his shoulders start to relax. He then talked with her for over an hour about how he felt persecuted for his beliefs, and the struggles he faced being a young Christian. His stories broke her heart, she could see that he was going through a lot and had no one to talk to about it.

She asked him why he didn't talk with Jason or any other men in the faith at the church about his problems, but he told her they were always too busy and some he didn't trust.

"Not everyone in the Church is saved—some only go for attention and others out of religious obligation. Jason was really the only one I trusted because he doesn't seem like he was out for the approval of others, but he is a person who is to himself. I never really knew how to approach him with things like this because he only ever handed me assignment's to do. He gives me a lot of advice about how to be a leader in the Church, but I don't tell him much about my personal life."

"He can be to himself, but I'm sure if you tell him what's on your heart he'll listen and give you some great advice." Audrey assured him. Then suddenly she remembered Jason's words that had caused a stir inside of her. Maybe they could be a help to Justin at his time of need.

"But you know…it's a beautiful thing being able to call yourself a child of the King. He loves you so much Justin, much more than you can ever imagine, and He sees the sacrifices you are going through for Him, and He's proud of you." She said.

"Thank you so much Ms. Audrey. That really encouraged me, because sometimes I feel like I'm just going day by day, without a purpose."

Audrey reached over the table and put her hand over Justin's. "You know what you should do?"

"What?" Justin looked down at her hand visibly shocked by her gesture.

"Live a little and don't be afraid to take risk—I mean this in a good way of course. Like for instance, the girl you like, you should just tell her. And even if she rejects you at least you won't have regrets or thoughts of "what if." And regarding those people who persecute you, love them because their sad people who don't know Jesus. Jesus went through the same thing. God will send you the right people in your life."

Justin paused. "You know, ever since you've come to the

church, I've seen a major positive change in the girls you mentor to, and now I see why." He smiled.

"Thank you." Audrey said, happy that she could be of some help to him.

On their way taking Audrey home Justin seemed like he was in a much better spirit. He even bobbed his head and sung along with the Christian songs being played over the radio station.

"You have a very nice voice Justin. You should sing in the young adult choir at the church."

"Thank you, but I don't like a lot of eyes being on me. I like teaching in the back with the children, with children their so eager to learn."

Audrey nodded her head. "I understand. I don't like attention either." Audrey remembered when she got up in front of the church and how nervous she was.

"You did really well with giving your testimony." Justin said as if he were reading her thoughts. "It was very moving."

"Thank you." She said.

They pulled into Jason's driveway. Before Audrey left his presence Justin thanked her for everything once again and he bid her a goodnight. Audrey came into the house exhausted and ready to go to sleep. When she got to the living room it took her a few minutes to notice Jason was sleeping on the couch with a book lying flat open on his chest. She tried tip toeing past him, but his eyes flew open when she made movement. When he saw her he rubbed his eyes and yawned.

"Where are you just now coming from? Did it take you and Justin that long to go through those books?"

"Well, yeah those are a lot of books, but he also took me out afterwards as a means of saying thank you for my help."

"You were out all night this late with Justin?" He raised his eyebrow.

"Yeah, is there something wrong with that?" Audrey began to wonder why Jason was prying. She never asked him what he and the duchess were up to.

"You were gone for so long I was just wondering where you were." He closed his book and stood up. "But I'm going to sleep now…goodnight."

There was something different about him that night Audrey couldn't pinpoint. When he was talking to her he could barely look at her in her face and he seemed irritated. She wondered had she did anything wrong to upset him, but being tired Audrey went to sleep and forgot about it.

The next couple of days though his strange behavior continued. He avoided her more than ever and he would seldom be home. When she did try talking to him he would say he was busy and go into his office.

One day when Audrey had some free time, which was something she was having less of as of recently, she went into the living room to watch a movie. She had been getting into Bible movies lately and was delighted to find that there was a variety of selections to watch. Lulu sat in her lap as she rubbed her fingers in her hair. During the credits of the movie Jason came out of his room and sat down on the other couch. She was surprised that he had even came out of the room to sit in her presence. At first she thought he was just going to sit there because he didn't say anything for a long time. He had his arms folded and watched as the credits played on the screen, but then after the credits were over with he looked over at Audrey for a brief second and then down at his lap.

"So I've been spending more time with Justin and he's been telling me some of his problems he's going through."

"Good, I'm glad he's opening up to you. I told him you would give him great advice."

Jason went on as if he didn't hear what she said. "He can't stop talking about you. He keeps saying how you're the nicest person he knows."

"That's sweet of him."

"I think he might like you."

Audrey just smiled and shook her head knowing that Jason was getting the wrong thoughts.

"What? Do you actually like him too?" Jason sat straighter in his chair. "Audrey he's a kid."

"I'm well aware of his age." Audrey said caught off guard from his bizarre accusation. "And no I don't like him, I was just being a help to him. Justin never gave me any indications that he liked me as well. I think you're getting his gratitude for me mixed up with something more."

"Are you sure there's nothing more." Jason asked firmly.

Jason was going too far if he thought Audrey would even think to like Justin. If Audrey didn't know any better she would think that Jason was being jealous. "Are you jealous?"

"Why would I have any need to be jealous? It's just that we don't need a scandal going on at the church between a teacher and her student. That wouldn't be a good image for the church Audrey."

"Well, I told you that you have nothing to worry about."

"Good." Jason got up to leave the room.

The rest of the day they didn't speak to one another at all. This was beginning to frustrate her because she didn't want the remainder of their time together to end off on such a bad note. Whatever she was doing to get under Jason's skin she wished she knew so that she could avoid it. All she wanted was for things to go back to the way they were. When they would watch movies together, eat together and even wash dishes together. She had grown accustomed to their life, but now that Rebecca was in the picture Jason had become a total different person. He was basically going back to the way he used to treat her when he first met Audrey, being cold and distant towards her.

Audrey knocked on the door to Mrs. Hanson's house. For the past couple of days she had been on her mind. Audrey remembered the kindness and hospitableness Mrs. Hanson had showed when she invited her and Jason to come over to her home. Since meeting her that day she didn't see her again, and Audrey felt bad that she didn't accept her up on her offer. Mrs. Hanson seemed liked a loving lady, and she also thought it would be a good idea to gain some cooking tips from her because she remembered Mrs. Hanson saying how much of a good cook she was. At least one time while staying with Jason did Audrey want to cook for him a good meal as a little way of showing him how much she appreciated him. She didn't want their hostility towards one another to continue any longer. Maybe making him a great meal would do the job of getting them back on good terms again.

When Mrs. Hanson opened the door it was all over her face how surprised and happy she was to see Audrey on the other end. She greeted her with a big hug and a wet kiss on the check. Mrs. Hanson invited Audrey into her home as if she was a family member and not a guest. Audrey found out that Mrs. Hanson was a lonely woman. She was a widow; her husband had passed away almost three years ago. They had been married for over fifty-eight years and she described him as being her best friend and soul mate. He was a reserved person, but he was kind to people and he had a sweet heart. He was a hardworking man and he would go out his way to make her happy. She said the day he died a part of her died as well, and that the only thing that kept her going was her faith in Jesus. Audrey could see even after his death Mrs. Hanson's heart still belonged to her husband.

They had no children together, although they did attempt to have a child many times. The first time ended with a miscarriage and then following that she just couldn't get pregnant. So Mrs. Hanson said she took it upon herself to love on other people's children, because she noticed that sometimes even though children could have parent's they can still be lonely and need love too.

She loved gardening, cooking and quilting. She was a person who enjoyed company, though not many came to visit her. Audrey could tell her visiting her brightened up Mrs. Hanson's day, and Audrey was happy she came.

When Audrey asked Mrs. Hanson about learning how to cook from her, Mrs. Hanson was elated. She immediately led Audrey to her spacious kitchen and they got to work making up something. Mrs. Hanson took her step by step through everything. She even gave her some of her cookbooks. By the end of their session Audrey felt like she could at least cook one decent meal for Jason that he would enjoy. What they prepared came out delicious. Mrs. Hanson's cooking was about as good as Jason's.

"I told you I can cook you up something mighty fine didn't I?" Mrs. Hanson smiled while collecting their empty plates.

"You most definitely are a great cook. I hope I can do as well as you." Audrey agreed.

"You will, just remember not to over season things or to overcook it. You'll do fine. And besides I can't take all of the credit today. After all, you did the cooking while all I did is simply coach you on what to do."

"Thank you Mrs. Hanson. Thank you for all of your help today."

"And thank you for coming to visit and old lady. You really

made my day special."

Before leaving Mrs. Hanson fixed her a plate to go and gave her another bear hug. She told Audrey to tell her *"brother"* hello.

While Jason was away running errands the next day Audrey prepared him a lavish meal. She carefully put together the main dish, side dishes and even dessert. She had to admit it to herself, after slaving in the kitchen for hours and even calling Mrs. Hanson's phone just to make sure she was doing everything right, Audrey believed she did an acceptable job. She dressed the dining room table up and made sure each plate had the same amount of food on it. She wanted everything to be just right for him. Hopefully this gesture would eliminate the unnecessary tension that had built between the two of them, that Audrey had no clue where had stemmed from.

Audrey heard Jason come through the front door and she became nervous. She was eager for him to try everything that she had prepared for him, yet she wanted him to like it as well. She went to meet him in the living room and when he saw her he looked at her briefly then kept walking to get to his room.

"Jason..." Audrey called out his name with hesitancy.

He turned his head around slowly to face her. From his expression it looked like he wasn't having a good day and that there was a lot on his mind.

Audrey put her head down feeling less confident in even asking him to have dinner with her now, but she swallowed her insecurity back and made eye contact with him again.

"I've prepared you a meal because I wanted to show you my thanks at least one time before leaving."

Jason looked away from her and then down at the floor.

"I've already ate." He said.

"Well…maybe we can eat together later?"

"I'll be busy later."

Audrey stood quiet. His words were like sharp knives ebbing away at her heart. She didn't know why Jason was acting so bitter towards her, but she couldn't take his icy attitude anymore.

"Is there something that I did to make you upset with me? Is it about Justin? I told you there is nothing between us."

Jason closed his eyes as if he were hurting from a headache, and then he opened them again. He still didn't look at Audrey directly. "It's nothing Audrey. I'm just tired today and I'd like to be left alone please."

Not allowing her to say anything else he went into his room. He was confined there for the rest of the day, leaving Audrey to eat the meal she'd made for him alone.

Chapter 16

Audrey stared at the picture in the hallway, not really comprehending what she should feel when looking at it. It was just a mess full of different colors, but for some reason while viewing it she forgot for a second what she'd been feeling for the past few days.

Lately she'd been having dreams about her past, provoking thoughts of shame inside of her. She didn't feel good enough and she felt condemned for the horrible actions she'd done. When she would read the Bible it said that God had forgiven her of her sins, but she didn't know if she had forgiven herself. She hated that she had those dreams. Audrey wanted to be free from them; she wanted to be free from everything entirely that had to do with her past. Maybe that's why Jason didn't want to be around her anymore, because he still saw her as her past, he still saw her as Jade. If that was the case, she couldn't blame him. She'd slept with married men and probably men who were even pastors. Thinking about it made her feel disgusted to be in her own skin.

Out of nowhere Jason appeared behind her. At first she thought he was just going to walk pass her and go on about his business, but then he stopped beside her. Audrey looked over at him and she could tell that he didn't sleep well, his eyes were dark underneath.

"I ate some of your food yesterday. You improved a great deal." He said with sincerity.

"Thank you." Audrey said taken off guard by his compliment.

She looked at the picture and remained quiet, not knowing what else to say because now things seemed awkward between the two of them. She didn't want to say something that might make him upset.

Jason let out a small cough. "By the way…I'm sorry for how I was treating you. I was going through something personally that I needed to deal with, but now I believe the situation is handled."

"Well, I'm glad you're feeling better." Audrey nodded.

Seconds passed of silence.

"Do you like this picture?" Jason asked. Audrey could tell he was trying to make conversation.

"It's nice. Gazing at it makes me forget about everything, because I'm too busy trying to figure out what I'm looking at." She chuckled.

Jason grinned for the first time in a long time and her heart smiled. "I used to think the same thing, but I've always loved art.

There's something about its silent meaning and how it can convey something different for each individual."

"I never thought of it that way." Audrey said.

Jason could see it in her eyes that Audrey was hiding her hurt. He hoped his behavior wasn't the cause of it. "What is it that you're trying to forget?"

Audrey paused. "I've been having those dreams again...I just want to be free from all of the mixed emotions I feel inside regarding my past. I feel like it's all bottled inside of me and I need for it to get out."

Jason remained quiet for a while. "Come follow me."

Audrey followed him curious to see where he was taking her. He led her pass the utility room and to a door she'd just realized she'd never noticed before. He opened the door and she went in behind him.

The room was filled with various drawings, an easel and painting materials. Audrey scanned around the room amazed at all of the beautiful paintings which were more vibrant than the one's displayed in the house.

"When I feel overwhelmed I come to this room and paint." Jason put his hands in his pockets.

"You paint?"

"Yeah, I'm not the best but I do it for fun or as a release from time to time. It's kind of a therapeutic hobby for me."

Jason showed Audrey some of his paintings and to Audrey's surprise they were much more beautiful then what Jason was putting on. Jason had a skill for anything he put his mind to. It amazed her how he was so artistic and good at everything he did.

Jason handed her a brush. "Here."

Audrey grabbed the brush in her hand. "I might not be as good at it like you are."

"It's ok. It's just for you to put out what you feel inside of you on this paper." He pointed to the blank sheet of paper.

Audrey began painting, mixing different colors. She didn't know what she was doing, but she took Jason's advice and just did what she felt. Halfway through Jason stopped her.

"Why aren't you using your favorite color?"

Audrey examined the picture, just realizing she was only using dark colors. Black and green were the primary colors, and the picture looked like a bunch of dark clouds hovering in the sky.

"I feel caged in, caged in my dark past." The words came out of her mouth before she could stop them.

Jason placed his hand over her hand that had the brush in it. His touch surprisingly calmed her yet excited her at the same time.

"Audrey, when you came into Christ your past was erased. God forgives you of your past and He wants you to experience the full newness you gain when you become a new creature in Him."

With his other free hand Jason flipped the page to another blank piece of paper and dabbed her brush on the blue paint. He then guided her hand to form the shape of a cloud.

"Experience that freedom again you felt like when you were a child." He let go of her hand.

Audrey could feel tears swelling in her eyes, but she blinked them back and continued to draw the clouds Jason had started for her. When she was finished she turned her body sideways to show Jason. In the process her paintbrush rubbed on Jason's check.

"Oh, I'm sorry." She grinned, trying to rub the paint from off of his check with her finger.

"I think you did that on purpose." Jason took his left hand, put it on the painting board and smeared paint all over Audrey's face.

Audrey took her brush and for a while she and Jason went back and forth putting paint on one another, running around the room like two little children playing a game of duck, duck goose. It was the most carefree Audrey had felt in such a long time. At the moment all she felt was joy and freedom.

Somehow Jason managed to trip over his feet and Audrey landed on top of him, their foreheads crashed together like waves hitting the shore.

"Ouch." Audrey sat up rubbing her forehead. "I'm sorry. I need to stop doing that." She pushed herself up about to get from off of Jason but he put his arm around her waist, keeping her straddled on top of his lap.

Stunned she sat still. His stare was so intense it sent shivers down her spine.

"No, that was my fault. I'm sorry." Jason gently rubbed his finger on her forehead and the only thing she felt was euphoria.

Now staring in his eyes she was sure she saw desire in them. His gaze fell from her eyes and then down to her lips. There was no space between them and she could feel his firm chest as he breathed in and out, his hands played up and down the spine of her back. Audrey felt everything inside of her flicker. If Jason leaned in to kiss her she knew that she would let him.

Jason blinked and then slightly shook his head swallowing. "I...I have to get ready for my date with Rebecca tonight."

Audrey felt like a brick had been thrown at her stomach. Was she only imaging everything that had just happened or did Jason really not feel anything for her? She stood to get from off of him and Jason went out of the room without saying anything else.

Audrey flushed the toilet and fixed herself up about to leave the stall to go back into the church service, until she heard some females enter into the restroom. Not in the mood to be sociable today she stayed inside of the stall until whoever they were left. A few minutes passed of the girls gossiping with one another. A thing Audrey was quickly finding out about some church people was that Justin was right about what he'd said about them. Many only came for attention and some just because they were raised in the church since birth.

Today these girls were talking about how they could make men do whatever they wanted and how they used them for their profit. They must've didn't know Audrey was there because they aired out all of their dirty laundry. Audrey was about to give them a surprise by revealing to them that she was in the restroom, but then she listened closer to the second voice that had just spoken. The more she listened the more she was certain it was Rebecca's voice.

"You know I had a date with him last night and it was horrible once again." She said to the other girl.

Audrey knew she was talking about Jason because he had left saying he was going on a date with her.

"I thought you said he was coming around." The girl responded.

"When I first came back to the church I thought he had developed a personality, but he's so boring. During our date the other night he noticed that I had on some Baby Phat jewelry and then he started talking about his cat the whole time and how it loves being scratched behind its ear or whatever. I hate cats."

They both giggled annoyingly.

"Well at least he's something to past the time with while you get over Blake."

"I guess, but I'm not going to lie, I miss Blake. If I could fly back to New York and be with him I would right now."

"Girl you need to get over him. He is the only man that you have gone this crazy about. What did he do to you?"

"Whatever Kenya, you fall in love and see if it's so easy to get over. But other than Blake there was David I used to have a major crush on him before I went away to move to go to college. I just wish I would've snatched up his brother before he got married. David is so fine with an outgoing personality."

Audrey felt her blood began to boil. So she was right all along about her suspicions regarding Rebecca. She never had pure intentions for Jason from the get go.

"The only reason I am continuing these dates is because I'm thinking maybe I can become the first lady when he becomes a pastor. Then I can become a stay at home wife."

"Girl I know that's right." She heard them give each other a high five.

It was taking everything in Audrey not to exit the bathroom stall and give her a piece of her mind. She couldn't believe all she had just heard and how conniving Rebecca was. If she wasn't saved she would've came out and had a few words with her for sure. But Audrey forced herself to remain calm and waited until they left.

She decided it was best to be honest with Jason and tell him everything she'd heard. Although Audrey didn't like Rebecca by far she wasn't so excited to let Jason know what she'd heard. She didn't want to see him hurt.

Audrey knocked on his office door that night and he told her to come in.

"Hi Jason." She came in slowly, dreading to tell him the news.

Jason kept typing whatever he was typing on his computer without looking her way. "Well…is there something you need from me?" He said after she didn't say anything.

Audrey took a deep breath before starting. "I was in the ladies restroom at church today and I overheard Rebecca saying a few things." Audrey paused trying to force herself to get out the rest. All she heard was Jason's fingers typing away on his keyboard. "I heard her tell her friend that she was only seeing you to become the first lady, but she had no real feelings for you whatsoever because she couldn't get over her ex from New York."

Jason stopped typing on his keyboard. He sat still without saying anything as he stared at his computer screen. Audrey stood feeling uncomfortable, not being able to read his expressionless face.

Jason rubbed between the bridge of his nose and shook his head. "Why would you make up something like that Audrey?"

"I'm not making anything up." She said, can't believing Jason was accusing her of lying to him. Did he trust her so little after all they'd been through? "I heard her say that you bored her with your continuous talk about Lulu and that she wanted to get with your brother…"

"Stop it! Just be quiet." Jason interrupted her. His voice was low, but his demeanor said it all. He was angry, but most of all she could see the disappointment in his eyes.

"Please get out so I can finish my work." Jason went back to typing.

Audrey left his office regretting her decision to tell Jason what she'd heard Rebecca say. If she would've known it would've caused him such discontent she would've rather kept it to herself.

Chapter 17

Audrey knocked on Trina's apartment door and waited for her to answer. She looked beside her at Cindy who was standing upright with a bright smile on her face, as always. Her face had gotten chubbier since she'd last seen Cindy. It looked like her baby was ready to arrive soon and very soon.

The both of them were coming to see Trina to offer her help and to tell her about their *Hope for Tomorrow* women's ministry. This was going to be Audrey's first time seeing her since she'd betrayed her, and she wasn't quite sure about how she was going to react when she saw Trina. Although she did forgive Trina, she still felt that is was wrong of her to snitch her whereabouts to Cash, putting her in danger. Before coming Audrey had explained to Cindy about what had happened and the history the two shared. Cindy told Audrey they didn't have to come if she didn't want to, but Audrey said it was ok because she did want to help Trina get out of prostitution and drugs. Audrey wanted Trina to experience the same freedom like she had done.

It took Trina awhile to open the door and when she finally did she appeared on the other end looking as thin as a rail. She looked no better than when Audrey saw her the last time.

When Trina saw Audrey her eye's immediately glazed and she started crying.

"Audrey, I'm so sorry, I'm so sorry." She could barely look at her in the face as she burst into more tears.

Remorse took hold of Audrey, and whatever ill will she might've felt for her vanished as she saw Trina's frail and weak frame hunched over in tears.

Audrey grabbed Trina in her arms and hugged her. "I forgive you Trina. I just want to see you do better than this, because there is so much more better than this." She squeezed her in her arms.

Audrey and Cindy stayed for a while as they explained to Trina what their ministry was about and how they would help her to get clean by being her accountability partners. They would help her look for a job and provide her with resources that would aid her in attaining a better life. Trina seemed like she was sincerely eager for a change. She told them how she was going on about three weeks without doing drugs, and this time she was serious about not going back to them.

Before leaving Audrey gave Trina her cell phone number and told her to call her if she needed anything at all. Audrey left feeling like things would be different this time, because believe it or not three weeks was the longest she'd ever heard Trina say she'd ever been without drugs since knowing her.

"You know Audrey, I admire you." Cindy said to her while driving her home.

"Really, you admire me? Why?" Audrey didn't think there was anything to be admired about her. Cindy was the one with the perfect life.

"After going through so much in your life, you don't seem like you were angry with God."

Audrey gazed out the window. "I was more so angry at myself than I was with God. I think I got that from my mom though. She blamed herself for a lot of things and felt like she was being punished all of time. I guess I'm being punished for my past too. I still sometimes think everything is my fault." Audrey said thinking about Jason's reaction when she told him about Rebecca's comments.

"Audrey, God doesn't hang our past around our necks. He forgives us and sets us free so we can live a life worth pleasing to Him. You've showed that you've been changed." Cindy smiled at her.

They drove in silence for a while longer. Audrey's mind kept wandering to Jason, and every time she thought about the way he was behaving her mood dampened.

"I've noticed you've been different lately. I don't mean to pry, but is there something wrong?" Cindy asked her. "You don't have to tell me if you don't want to. It's just I really do see you as my sister now and if there is anything I can do to help you I will."

Audrey could tell that Cindy was being sincere with her concern. Since knowing Cindy she'd always kept her word and Audrey had never heard her once gossip about anyone. Maybe opening up to someone about it would help to alleviate the heaviness she felt on her heart.

"I...I'm in love with Jason." She spilled.

Cindy's eyes widened. "Well...I could've told you that."

"What?" Audrey said surprised.

"I think everyone can see the chemistry you two share. You bring out of Jason what nobody else could. He's opened up more and he does things with passion now."

"It seems like everyone keeps telling me that, but I don't see much of a change I'm doing. He's head over heels for Rebecca and I'm just getting in his way."

"What makes you think he likes Rebecca?"

"Well, because he's seeing her now."

"You know...when I see those two together at church he doesn't seem so happy to be around her. He doesn't seem nearly as happy with her as he is when I see him with you."

Audrey looked over at Cindy. "Really?"

"Really." Cindy nodded.

Hearing what Cindy said made her feel that maybe she had made some positive influence in Jason's life, but at the same time she was still confused with why Jason was being so distant towards her. Even before she'd told him about Rebecca he was acting this way.

Jason sat in his office, staring at the computer screen, but not reading what was on it. He wondered where Audrey had gone off to and what was taking her so long to get back home. Jason shook his head. Why was he always thinking about her? Even after she'd come into his office accusing Rebecca of saying such heinous things, Audrey was still the topic that ran across his mind constantly, every minute of the day. It irritated him to no end.

His phone vibrated and he checked the text message that'd just come in. It was Rebecca and it read *"I miss you."*

Rebecca had never sent such an affectionate text like this to him before. Usually they just discussed where they were going to meet up next or maybe talk about the weather. When it came to conversing with Rebecca Jason found it to be difficult. Unlike before she'd left to go to New York she was different. She didn't have the interest she once held for ministry. Instead she talked a lot about the latest fashion or celebrity news, things that Jason didn't find remotely interesting so he'd just listen to her. Maybe she wanted to take things to another level with their relationship instead of it being just a friendship.

Jason texted her back *I miss you too.*

After a few seconds she replied with a smiley face. *I knew you did. When I come back to New York we can be together.*

Jason exited from the text without responding back, realizing that Audrey had been right. For some reason he didn't even feel angry nor was he surprised, but he was more so relieved. He knew God had allowed her to text the wrong person for a reason.

"Can you wait here for a minute? I have to go give these books to Justin so he can add them the children's book collection." Audrey said before Jason had backed up to leave the church the next day.

Jason nodded his head and Audrey got out of the car. He'd wanted to tell her he was sorry for not believing her, but he couldn't muster to tell her because he felt embarrassed for the way he'd treated her. Audrey he knew was only looking out for him and he had responded in such a harsh way to her. He decided he would tell her when she got back inside of the car.

Audrey quickly walked to the children's classroom to find Justin before he left that day. When she entered the classroom he was already packing up to go.

"Good, I came just in time. I was meaning to tell you I had purchased a few books to donate to the children's ministry." Audrey looked down at the books in her hand just noticing she had left one behind in the car. "Oh, hold on a second, I left one in the car. I'll run right back." She said turning to leave.

"Wait." Justin gently grabbed her by her wrist. He looked at her as if all his breath were stuck in his throat. "Remember when you told me to live a little and to take risk?"

"Yeah." Audrey said not sure of where this was going.

Suddenly Justin lowered his head to her mouth and kissed her. Not expecting him to do that, she remained frozen from the complete shock. Before she could back away from him her eyes fell to the entrance of the room and she saw Jason staring wide eyed at the both of them. She pushed him away from her and Justin followed to where her eyes were located.

When he noticed Jason Justin immediately became stiffened. Nobody said anything for a few seconds. Jason glared at the both of them like they had committed the worse sin ever.

"Ja—" Audrey started, but Jason held up his hand to silence her.

"You left behind a book." He placed the book on a nearby desk and then walked out of the room.

Audrey hurried to follow him. She came out to the parking lot expecting to find Jason had left her behind, but to her surprise he was in the car waiting for her.

For the whole ride they didn't say anything and to be honest from the look on his face Audrey thought it would be wise to let him cool off. The frown on his face was so sharp that she could see the lines that'd formed on his forehead.

When they got inside of the house Jason made his way across the living room to go into either his room or office, but then he stopped midway. He turned to face Audrey and she looked away not being able to hold his angry gaze.

"Why did you do it Audrey, huh? I thought you said there was nothing going on between the two of you."

"There isn't. Justin just suddenly kissed me out of the blue and I was too taken off guard to push him away, but I was about to before I even saw you in the doorway."

Jason calmed himself down, feeling way too angry than what he thought he should. But at the same time he had a right to his anger. If a scandal broke loose because of this that would be bad press for the church. How could Audrey kiss Justin? The more the image of them kissing reappeared in his head the more enraged he became.

"I thought you were through with that dirty lifestyle. Now you're trying to take the innocence of a little boy?"

Audrey processed what he'd said, at the same time not believing what he'd just said. "Are you serious Jason? Is that how you see me? And before you answer I would advise you to think carefully about your response first."

Jason could see he had struck a nerve. The deepest part of him believed she was telling him the truth, but a fraction of him still felt upset and he couldn't help how he felt at the moment. So instead of saying anything he might've regretted later he just left to go inside of his room.

A few hours later Jason received a phone call from Justin on his cell phone. Justin explained to him that the fault was all on him and Audrey had nothing to do with it. He told Jason the reason why he'd done what he did was because he'd been going through a lot lately and had gotten his emotions all confused up. He became so remorseful over the phone that Jason thought he heard him sniffling on the other end.

Jason told him that all was forgiven and that he would be spending more time with him, and that he himself was sorry for neglecting him in his personal life. Instead of adding more to his stressful load he wanted to be a friend to take some of the heavy weight off. At the end of the conversation Justin asked Jason could he apologize to Audrey for him because she wasn't answering any of his phone calls and Jason agreed.

When he hung up the phone with Justin Jason left his room and knocked on Audrey's closed door. She told him he could come and he pushed the door open.

"You were right about Rebecca, and I know you didn't initiate the kiss with Justin. I'm sorry." He said.

Audrey looked at him with disappointment and Jason felt ashamed.

"I forgive you." She said. "But could you tell me why you've been treating me the way you have lately? I don't like it."

"It's just..." Jason tried to think of why he was acting harsh towards her as well, but nothing could come to his mind. He didn't know why he himself was behaving like the way he was. "It's just a lot that has been going on, but I promise I won't treat you that way again."

"I hope not." Audrey petted Lulu who was lying on her bed. "Time really does fly. You know I only have exactly a month left here. Cindy's been helping me look for an apartment. There's this really nice one, which is also affordable that I'm thinking about signing with next week."

The thought of Audrey leaving was somehow strange to Jason. "That's good." He stood in her doorway not sure exactly what else to say.

"Are you up for a movie tonight? I looked up a good light comedy movie and its rated PG." Audrey added.

"I think a movie sounds good." Jason nodded.

Throughout the movie this time Jason would join in on the laughter. Lulu got so tired of the both of them that she settled for the other couch. Being with him again like this Audrey felt glad things were back to normal. She had missed spending time with him and she knew she would miss it even more when the time came for her to move out.

Chapter 18

The next morning Jason had found himself and Audrey had fallen asleep on the couch together. Audrey was lying in his arms sound asleep looking peaceful as she did so. Her smooth skin glistened in the early morning sunlight that streamed through the windows. Jason rubbed his finger on her cheek and her left eye twitched. He quickly removed his finger and instead watched her so he wouldn't wake her up.

He felt warm and relaxed with her in his arms, and he didn't want her to get up. But then again he shouldn't be feeling the way he did. Jason didn't understand these feelings, but most of all he didn't like the feelings he had for her. Over and over again he told himself he didn't like Audrey, but part of him felt like he was beginning to develop a deeper affection for her.

Jason shook his head. No, that couldn't be it. If it was anything it was because she was like a sister to him that he'd come to care about. Yeah, that had to be it.

Audrey woke up on the couch to the smell of breakfast being cooked. Lulu licked her toes and she giggled. After brushing her teeth she went into the kitchen to find Jason putting scrambled eggs on the plates. She stopped herself from smiling, thanking God that before leaving she could enjoy Jason's fine cooking once again.

"I sort of already knew you were right about Rebecca before even receiving that text. I think I was just sticking on to the old perfect image I had of her before she went away to New York." Jason said after they sat down at the dining table and ate their breakfast together.

Audrey nodded her head. "I understand. Sometimes we have images in our mind of what we want a person to be like, but then they turn out to be a completely different person." Audrey thought of Cash and how he deceived her with his gentleman like image.

"She came up to me yesterday before leaving church asking me did I want to go out on another date. I told her no because I don't live in New York."

Both Jason and Audrey chuckled together. Then Audrey looked at him with the most beautiful smile that made his heart melt. "You know she missed out a great guy." She told him.

Jason thanked her and Audrey could've sworn that she saw him blushing, but before she could get a good look at him he took another mouthful of his scrambled eggs.

"Hey, can I talk to you for a moment?" Gordon Thompson approached Audrey through the church's hallway one day while she was running an errand.

"Sure, what can I do for you?" Audrey stopped walking.

Gordon stepped closer to her as if he wasn't already close to her enough as it was, backing her into the wall behind her. He did a quick look around before his eyes met hers again.

"So I was wondering if you and Jason were seeing one another."

She wanted to bluntly ask him what did that have to do with him, but instead she remained courteous. "No, we're not, but I don't think that's any of your concern." She said politely.

"Ok, ok." Gordon grinned. "I've been silently keeping my eye on you and I just wanted to know if I can take you out sometime." His face showed his true intentions. He had the same look in his eyes the men on Lankford Avenue showed Audrey whenever they paid for her for their pleasure.

"No, thank you. I'm not interested." She said firmly, and then she tried to go on about her business, but Gordon wouldn't move out of her way.

"Are you serious? You're denying me?" His cockiness seeped

from his tone.

"Yes, I'm serious. Now if you would let me get back to my work I would appreciate that."

"Well, what if I paid you? I know you can't be that expensive."

Audrey felt her hand shake. Did Gordon mean what she thought he meant?

"I told you I don't want to go out with you." She attempted to keep her cool.

"I'm not talking about going out for dinner sweetheart. I'm talking about something else." He licked his lips.

Audrey closed her eyes and counted to three, praying that God would give her grace on how to handle the situation. She opened her eyes and smiled up at him.

"I don't live that lifestyle anymore. If you want to degrade women I suggest you ask the Lord to truly come into your heart. You should learn how to value a woman then maybe—just maybe one would find you slightly attractive."

Gordon stood straight with a frown, visibly upset about what she'd just said.

"Well, I don't know who would value a woman like you. You're still a filthy tainted whore, whose spread your legs open to numerous of different men. No pure and decent man would ever be crazy enough to want you as a housewife."

Before Audrey knew it she had slapped him right in his face and the rest was history as he howled in pain.

After checking his text message from Audrey Jason hurried into the church's office where she said she'd be waiting.

When he went into the office Audrey was sitting down, with her arms crossed furious. Gordon was standing and Charles Hunt, an elderly man who was another volunteer at the church was also present.

"I witnessed this young lady slap this man when I was walking in the hallway to go to the restroom, but other than that I don't know what else transpired before then." Charles said. "We are waiting on Pastor James to come deal with the situation. He is on his way after he's done teaching."

"Thank you Mr. Hunt." Jason said. He looked over at Gordon who had a smug look on his face.

"Hmph, it figures she would call you to try to get her out of this. But that Jezebel woman has crossed the line. She slapped me and I'm pressing charges against her for it." Gordon dramatically placed his hand over his lightly bruised check where Audrey had slapped him.

Jason refrained himself from rolling his eyes at his over the top scene. "Before we make any decisions we need to hear both sides of the story."

"Excuse me, but are you the head pastor?" Gordon huffed. "I think I will wait until Pastor James gets here, thank you."

"Well, I'll tell him my side of the story then." Audrey interjected. "This man," she pointed to Gordon. "Came up to me in the hallway and basically insulted me, calling me a whore after I rejected his offer to pay me to go out with him."

Jason saw it in her eyes that she wanted to cry, but she held it back. He looked over at Gordon who just stood with a smirk. Jason wanted to slap that smirk from off of his face. He didn't even show an ounce of remorse for his actions.

"Don't tell me you believe what she's saying." Gordon said after Jason frowned over at him.

"Yes I do believe what she's saying."

"Are you kidding me? I wouldn't touch that Jezebel woman with a ten foot pole." Gordon said disgusted.

Before Jason knew it his body was walking over to Gordon by a will of its own. Then the door to the office opened and Pastor James stepped in. Immediately his presence was known and everyone got silent as they looked his way.

"I think I've heard enough." He said sternly.

"You...you heard everything?" Gordon said looking sick in the face.

"Yes I did. And I believe you owe this young woman an apology."

When the meeting was done and over with Gordon got sat down from his ministry duties and he was forced to apologize to Audrey for his unacceptable behavior. Fortunate for him Audrey decided not to press any charges against him.

The next day after they were finished watching a movie Audrey turned to face Jason. The question she wanted to ask him had been burning at her heart, but she felt reluctant to ask him about it.

Jason turned to her. "What? Is there something on my face?" He rubbed his hand over his cheek.

Audrey smiled from his dorky yet appealing charm. "No." She said.

"Then what is it?" Jason asked her after she wouldn't stop looking at him.

Audrey took a deep breath. "Do you think that what Gordon said about me is true?"

"Not at all, you should ignore his words."

Audrey played with her fingers, contemplating should she ask him her next question. Since she only had two more weeks to stay with him what did she have to lose?

"Would you ever want to date me?" Her words came out in more of a whisper, but she knew Jason had heard her because his face went uncomfortably still.

He remained quiet for so long that Audrey didn't think he was going to answer.

"You're like a sister to me." He finally said. "Why would I want to date you?"

"Is it that I'm like a sister to you, or is it that you just don't think I'm good enough for you?"

"Audrey, what is this all about?" Jason said tiptoeing around the question.

"Answer my question Jason. Do you still see me as my past?" Although he didn't want to say it looking into his eyes Audrey already knew the answer, and it nearly broke her heart.

"Oh…I get it. Jesus can forgive me, but I'm way too dirty to ever be really seen as pure, right?"

"Audrey…I didn't say that."

"You didn't have to say it." She got up.

"Where are you going?"

"I'm going to meet Cindy. We had something to do today."

"Well, let me take you. I had to go to the church for a meeting with my dad anyways."

"No, I'll just take the bus." She left before he could say anything else.

In the meeting with his dad Jason couldn't stop his leg from twitching the whole time. His mind had Audrey running through it on nonstop replay that he couldn't concentrate on what his dad was saying.

"My boy…are you listening to me?" Pastor James voice vibrated in his ears.

Jason sat up straight in his chair and focused his attention on him. "I'm sorry."

Pastor James folded his hands together before continuing. "What I really wanted to call you into my office to tell you is that…I'm proud of you son."

Jason didn't attempt to hide his shock and Pastor James must've noticed it.

"I know I don't tell you those words much and I apologize for that." He paused. "Your friend Audrey is a great woman. I've seen the change in you since you've invited her to church. When she gave her testimony that day of how you helped her change her life around it showed me how you do care for the lost."

"Well, thank you sir. The credit goes to God." Was all Jason could say because he was so floored by his dad's kind words.

"You know…you can call me dad or father, whichever one you'd prefer to call me." His dad smiled, it was the first time Jason had seen him smile at him in a long time.

"That lamp was your mothers." He looked over at the wicker table.

"I didn't know that." Jason said softly.

"The thing I regret the most is pushing her away from me and putting ministry first. I should've been there to help her in her most times of need. You're mother wasn't a bad person. She loved you. The day before she died she called me to tell me she would be keeping you for the whole summer break. She said she wanted to make things right with you."

The way his dad was talking to him right now was how a father would to his son. Something Jason had missed out from him his entire life. He was so used to seeing the business and stern side of him, but right now his dad was vulnerable, opening up his heart to Jason, and Jason felt himself getting emotional and he didn't know why.

"If you want the position of executive pastor it's yours. I was always going to give it to you, but I wanted you to be ready first. I didn't want you to close other people out like I had done for so long. I wanted you to be better than me."

Jason nodded his head because it was the only thing he could think to do.

"By the way, was your lady friend staying in your home with you this whole time?" His dad went back to talking in his authoritative tone again.

Jason nervously sat straighter in his chair, knowing he couldn't lie to him. "Yes sir, but I assure you there was no fornication that took place. I was only helping her with a place to stay, she is actually moving out soon. I take my relationship with God very seriously." His dad stared at him with his beady eyes as if he were trying to discern if the words Jason was telling him were true or not.

"Besides…wasn't it you, dad, who asked me when was the last time I ever opened up my home to a stranger? I was simply putting what you taught me into practice." Jason felt his leg tapping.

His dad looked at him for a while longer, and then suddenly he began to chuckle, taking Jason by a great surprise. Jason chuckled himself to lessen the nervousness he felt.

"Son, I believe you. I know that you are a faithful man of God. I've seen the upright life you live for Him. Just make sure if she is the one to go ahead and do things the right way by marrying her first, you have my blessings if you do."

Before Jason could say anything his father stood and gave him a long hug and told him that he loved him.

After Jason left his office while passing by the conference room his eyes caught sight of Cindy. He went inside searching the room for Audrey, but couldn't find her. Cindy was in the office alone going through some papers. When she noticed Jason was in the room she looked over at him and smiled.

"Hey Jason. How are you?"

"I'm good thanks how are you?"

She put her hand on her belly. "Oh, David and I are just about ready for this baby to arrive, but other than that I'm good. Are you looking for someone?"

"I'm looking for Audrey. She said you two had a meeting."

"We didn't have one that I know of. I actually haven't seen her any today."

"Are you sure?"

"Yeah."

Jason turned to leave the room to give Audrey a call on her cellphone.

"Jason." Cindy called out.

He turned back to face her.

"Don't let her get away. Everyone can see the impact she's made in your life. Don't let fear get in the way of your happiness."

When Jason got home he didn't find Audrey there. Worried he called her phone again, but she still didn't pick up. Was what Cindy said true? Was he just afraid to fully open up himself to Audrey and that's why he was hiding his feelings. He had to admit, Audrey had been the only woman he was ever so comfortable to be around. Just being able to be with her was one of the most satisfying things to him, and he couldn't stand the thought of her moving away from him.

It wasn't her past that scared him anymore, it was the feelings he had for her which were beginning to consume him that did. He was always so used to being in control of everything, but the feelings he held for Audrey was one thing he couldn't contain from growing. And now more than ever he felt at a loss of control because at this very moment the realization hit him like a crashing tsunami, he loved Audrey. He loved her and he couldn't deny it anymore.

By the time it was approaching dark outside Jason had become extremely worried. He'd even called her job and they said she didn't come in at all that day, and she wasn't on schedule to come in either. Before resulting to calling the police he decided maybe he should text her.

Come home, I'm worried about you and I miss you so much that it hurts.

Jason texted, but then quickly deleted it. Noticing that he had actually sent it instead he panicked. He didn't mean to send it and he had only texted it on a whim. Jason bit into his fist, staring frozen at the screen as if that would make the text magically disappear.

Audrey came through the door from visiting Mrs. Hanson's and saw Jason standing in the living room looking at the phone in his hand. He was so distracted he didn't even hear her come in. She had just got his text and as soon as she read if she didn't know what to think of it. Her first thought was maybe he'd texted the wrong person, but at the possibility of it really being meant for her she rushed home to find out.

"Jason." She said.

Jason looked over at her startled. After he peered at his phone again he put it inside of his pocket.

"Are you ok?" He asked her shuffling his feet from side to side.

"I'm fine." She paused. "Did you mean what you put in that text message to me?"

He paused before answering. "Yes…yes I did." Jason took a deep breath. "And before I lose the courage to say it I wanted to tell you something that has been on my heart. Audrey, you…you dug out all the ugliness that I didn't have a clue that was deep inside of me. When I first met you I didn't know compassion, but you taught me that. You made me see the beauty of life and God's power of redemption. You're beautiful not only on the outside, but the inside too. And you are good enough, maybe even too good enough for me. After all you've been through you still have enough space in your heart to love and care for others more than you do for yourself. I've come to the realization that I don't want to let you go. I love you and I want you to stay here with me. At first it was under the pretenses of being my long lost sister, but now I would like it as the reality of you being my wife."

Audrey's breathed nearly stopped. Did she really just hear Jason say he loved her? Was he asking her to marry him? Being speechless from amazement she couldn't even form her mouth to say anything.

Jason closed the space between them and cupped her chin in his hand. He seemed hesitant and nervous at first, but then he leaned in and slowly pressed his lips on hers. Something so wonderful went off inside of Audrey she couldn't even explain. Audrey felt his body heat become one with hers. He wrapped his arms firmly around her and she drowned into his warm embrace. Jason's lips fluidly caressed hers, Audrey submitted to his flow relishing every moment of it. He was so gentle yet every move he made exploring her lips with his made her weak in the knees, causing her body to lean more into his chest.

Suddenly Lulu rubbed in between their legs and they both broke their kiss, which had left Audrey breathless.

Jason smiled and looked down at Lulu. "Don't worry Lulu, you're not going anywhere either."

Jason turned his gaze back to Audrey. She smiled and put her arms around his shoulders thinking she must've been in a perfect dream she didn't want to wake up from. When she looked into Jason's eyes she saw her new future with him, a future of love, joy and freedom, with God being the center of it all.

A MESSAGE FROM THE AUTHOR

I would like to thank all of the readers so much for taking the precious time out of your lives to read my novel. I hope that I can make more characters for you as I grow in my gifting. If you would like to hear more of this story let me know. And you can also find more updates on my website at

shaniquasnowden.com

or

facebook.com/ShaniquaSnowden